D1156286

THE ROAD TO KIP'S COVE

Illustrated by WILLIAM WHEELER

THE MACMILLAN COMPANY

THE ROAD
TO KIP'S COVE

Lyn Cook

OF CANADA LIMITED - TORONTO

Also by Lyn Cook

THE BELLS ON FINLAND STREET

THE LITTLE MAGIC FIDDLER

REBEL ON THE TRAIL

JADY AND THE GENERAL

THE MAGICAL MISS MITTENS

SAMANTHA'S SECRET ROOM

THE SECRET OF WILLOW CASTLE

Third printing, 1965

Reprinted, 1973

ISBN 0-7705-0061-7

PRINTED IN CANADA

For our Kip and Deb
and for
Anna Kitchen's grandchildren
descendants of
William White

Contents

1. A Surprise for Summer   1
2. An Indian Boy and Kip's Cove   15
3. A Ghost or Two   33
4. A Noise in the Night and a New Job   50
5. To Find the Frenchman's Gold   72
6. Cave in the Mountain   87
7. Swimming Lessons and Tales of the Mohawks   99
8. A Day with the Indians   112
9. A Dog Named Scout and a Red Canoe   124
10. The Canoe Adventure Begins   136
11. A Man in the Dark   144
12. Midnight on Spook Island   156
13. Birthday in a Barn   165
14. A High Wind and an Accident   174
15. Scout's Gone!   184
16. Kanati, Lucky Hunter   198
17. Edna's Ghost at Last   208
18. Welcome Home Skipper!   217

Lakefield

Nassau

Peterborough

TRENT CANAL
LOCK SCENE

Trent River

Heely Falls

Trent River

Ourse
River

Hastings.

Campbellford

Otonabee River

Campbelltown

Serpent Mounds Park

Hiawatha
Reserve

Kent
Creek

Rice Lake

Wilson Island

Tick Island
Spook Island

Gore's Landing

Frank

DESERONTO FERRY

Trento

Carrying P

OLD MILL
AT HASTINGS

WHITE CHAPEL

GLENORA-ADOLPHUSTOWN
FERRY

HAUNTED HOUSE
AT STIRLING

WISHING TREE

HAY BAY
CHURCH

Stirling

oss
Rawdon Creek.

Napanee

Belleville

Tyendinaga
Reserve   Deseronto

Bay of Quinte

Hay Bay

Hay Bay Church

Adolphustown

White Chapel   Glenora

Lake on the Mountain

Picton

Bloomfield

West Lake   Wishing-tree.

"Kip's Cove."

East Lake

Sandbanks

Little Sandy Bay

Outlet Provincial Park

Salmon Point

Lake Ontario

W. wheeler '61

THE ROAD TO KIP'S COVE

1. A Surprise for Summer

"I'm home!" Kip bounded in the back door and let it slam shut behind him.

"So I hear." Edna stood at the top of the short stairway, hands on hips.

Kip made a rueful face. "Oh, sorry. I did say I'd try to remember not to slam it the next time, didn't I?"

"A good many next times it seems to me," Edna said. "How did it go today?"

"Oh, fair, I guess." Kip set his lunchbox on the kitchen table. "But it didn't work out about taking the lunch. I still didn't meet anybody who'd come over after school."

"You will," Edna assured him. "Give yourself time. You've only been here a week."

Kip opened the refrigerator door. "Isn't there any pop?"

"Only milk after school. Those were your mother's orders. Remember the teeth," Edna said. "But you can have a cookie or two."

1

"Just two? I'm starved!"

"You always are," Edna smiled. "And if you're starved at eleven, what are you going to be when you're fourteen?"

"Six feet tall like Dad," Kip grinned. "That's what I'm working on now." He sat down at the table. "When are they coming home, anyway?"

"Tonight, after supper, I think. You'd better get your homework done now, and then we can sit and listen to what they did, if they get home before bedtime." Edna folded up the ironing board.

"Where were they going, Edna?"

"I'm not quite sure. Somewhere east of here, from what your father said. I think they just wanted to wander without too much definite in mind. Your mother was tired after all the business of the moving, and Laurie's wedding, of course. It'll do her good to get away for a few days."

Yes, Kip remembered, the house had been in an uproar for months over his sister's wedding. It seemed funny to think of her living so far away in the States. "I wonder if they'll bring me anything home," he said.

Edna eyed him disapprovingly. "Is there anything you haven't already got? If there is, you can be sure your mother will get it for you."

It was true. If ever he wanted something he knew the person to approach was his mother. She would always give in to his wheedling and somehow she managed to persuade his father and the point was won. The only thing it hadn't worked with was the dog, but there was no use even mentioning that any more.

"I haven't got everything, Edna," Kip said. "You know how much I want a transistor radio."

Edna raised her eyebrows. "Is that all you want? My, oh, my! That hardly seems like anything at all. I'll run out and get you one right now!"

"Well, they aren't very expensive, Edna." Kip pushed his

science book aside. "You can get a really good one for about thirty dollars."

"Thirty dollars!" Edna said. "Just remember, young man, that's a week's wages for me!"

"Is it?" Kip was always a little surprised when the question of Edna's being paid arose. She had been with them for so many years, since he had been born and his mother had first been ill, that she had become a natural part of the family. He often felt closer to her than he felt to his parents, mainly, he supposed, because they spent so much time together. Edna was a born story-teller. Some of his happiest moments as a child had been spent in the kitchen with her, listening to tales of her home in an eastern farming community. That had been in the big old house they had just left behind. "Edna, I wish we'd never had to move," he said suddenly.

"Well, I miss the old place, too," Edna confessed. "But it was too big for us after Laurie left. Your father thought a change to the suburbs might do your mother good, too, and I think it will." She surveyed her domain proudly. "And you wouldn't get me to trade in this new kitchen on anything."

But that, Kip thought, is just why I don't like it as well. The newness. His first home had been huge and rambling, in an older part of the city. There were three floors of spacious, old-fashioned rooms and many intriguing cupboards under winding stairways where he could hide in secret when he wanted to be alone. Here, in the new sprawling ranch-type house, all the rooms were on one floor. There was only the panelled recreation room down a short flight of stairs where he could seek solitude with his books and his thoughts.

"Besides," Edna went on, "I can't understand why a boy like you doesn't love it here, with that ravine right behind the house. If I were you, I'd be making forts and tree houses and all sorts of things down there."

"What's the good of a ravine if there's nobody to go down there with me?" Kip wanted to know. "If Brian and Mike and some of the kids from Holloway Street were only here now, then we'd really have ourselves a time."

"Do you mean to say there aren't any boys around here your own age?"

Kip shrugged his shoulders. "There are some maybe, but they have their own gang, and they just don't want me in it, I guess."

Then suddenly he brightened. "Anyway," he said, "it's only a month and a half till summer holidays, and we'll be going up north! John and Peter will be there and we'll have a super time." He did not notice the peculiar glance that Edna cast in his direction as he bent his head over his arithmetic book.

Later, down in the recreation room, he played with the hockey game while Edna washed the supper dishes. He tried to imagine Mike or Brian working the small levers at the other end of the gaily coloured rectangle which held the miniature figures. He even wished at this point that there had been a younger member of the family to play with. He had agreed with Mike whole-heartedly when the latter had complained about his brother being a nuisance, but at the moment a nine-year-old companion in the house would have been sheer delight. He had always been like an only child, anyway, coming as he had so much later in his parents' lives, with his sister Laurie ten years older, and yet he had not noticed it to any degree until now. When he was very small, there had always been Edna and whatever bevy of small companions she could muster in the house and the small hedged garden. And then, as he grew, there had been Mike and Brian, his favourites because they never challenged his leadership. They admired the big spare room where they came to play in their younger days, and to form their "club" as they grew older. They liked, too, the multitude of games that were stacked on the shelves of his room. "Gee," Brian had said on one occasion, "can you just ask for anything and get it?"

"Sure," Kip had said with a little swagger. "Almost anything, anyway. My mother likes me to get things."

The statement had puffed him up immeasurably at the time, as had the dog-like devotion of his two friends to his every whim. Neither did him any good now. He was alone, and where he would find two pals like Mike and Brian he did not know.

"The car's coming in the driveway!"

He heard the crunch of the tires on the gravel as soon as he heard Edna's voice. As he ran up the steps, his mother came in the front door, her thin face relaxed and smiling.

"Hello, dear." She kissed him quickly. "How did everything go?"

"Okay." Kip had not ducked swiftly enough to escape the kiss. His mother must know that he was getting too old for that sort of thing now. "Did you have a good time?"

"Wonderful!" Mrs. Brooks took off her coat and hat. Her husband came in as she opened the cupboard door.

"Where's Edna?" Mr. Brooks asked.

"Out here in the kitchen brewing you up some coffee!" Edna called. She poked her head round the door. "We have to have a welcome-home party, you know."

"Did you keep this young man in line?" Mr. Brooks nodded shortly towards Kip.

Kip managed a half smile but he felt his father's sternness in the question. His 'father was always serious, not gay and laughing and pliable like his mother.

But he smiled quietly now as Edna replied, "Oh, I managed somehow, with the threat of a broom handle and no chocolate cake for supper." She winked at Kip. "Didn't I, skipper?"

"You know you never had to threaten at all," Kip laughed. "We got along fine." He turned to his mother. "Where did you go and what did you see?" He would never think of asking his father the question. It was always his mother who could not wait to share her adventures.

"We went down to Cornwall to see Aunt Mary first, Kip,

and on the way back we did a little driving around the Bay of Quinte." She glanced quickly at her husband as they all sat down in the living-room. "We found something there we think you're going to like, Kip, a surprise for summer."

"Oh?" Kip said.

"Don't tell him now, Bet, until the thing is completely settled," Mr. Brooks warned. "We don't know if it's going to be possible yet."

"What's going to be possible?" Kip glanced, puzzled, from one to the other.

Edna tapped his arm. "You heard what your father said, you have to wait a little to find out."

"But can't you tell me now?" Kip was exasperated.

"Christopher!" He knew there was a reprimand coming from his father as soon as he heard his proper name. "When will you learn that what we say we mean? You will know when we think it's time for you to know and not before. And if I find you pestering your mother about this, you'll be punished."

So that was that, Kip thought sullenly. Here was one secret that would remain a secret. His father had a habit of meaning what he said.

"It's a beautiful part of the country down there," his mother broke in gaily. "Miles and miles of pasture land and farming country, and stretches of the bluest water!"

"Isn't that where the sand dunes are?" Edna asked. "I've seen pictures of them."

"That's right." Mr. Brooks' voice was quiet again. "They're near Bloomfield. And the whole area is a gold mine for anyone interested in pioneer times and settlements."

"History!" Kip snorted. "Who wants to learn about that? We get enough of it in school!"

"By the looks of that mark on the last report card, young man, I'd say you didn't," Edna said wryly. "It might do you good to go and absorb a little atmosphere."

"That's what we had in mind." Mr. Brooks refilled his coffee cup. "We had hoped, if all goes well, to take Kip down there in a week or two, but of course, if he isn't interested . . ."

"Oh, I'm interested!" Kip was angry with himself. To think his own words had robbed him of a week-end away. "I'd love to go, Dad, and see everything. Please don't change your mind. It's just learning all those dates and things I don't like. But if we could see places where people lived in the old times, that would be different."

"Well, we'll see." Mr. Brooks lit his pipe. "I'm expecting a letter some time this week, and we'll know for sure then if we have anything definite to go down for."

Anything definite to go down for. Kip mulled over the words later in his room. He could not imagine what they meant. What had his father and mother done while they were away? Discovered a long-lost relative? Invested in a new business? Bought something as a surprise for him? Of the three the last seemed most likely, and then he wondered what it could be. The possibility of a dog occurred to him with a shock of delight. It was something he had always wanted and his father had steadfastly refused to buy. He had said that the city home, with its small garden, was no place to keep an animal. But out here, where there was a rolling back lawn reaching to the wooded ravine, what could be more perfect? He could not see his father deliberately setting out with a dog in mind, but perhaps they had come across a litter of puppies in their travels, and his mother had persuaded him. The more he thought about it, the more convinced he became that this was the answer. What a friend he would have then! There would be no need to worry about another until they went north when school was over. He and his dog would be the best of pals. They would go roaming the ravine together looking for rabbits. He would build a fort and he and his dog would hide out in it against the world. Every afternoon after school his dog would come running down the road to meet him, and lick his hands and face with the joy of seeing his master again. He could almost feel the tongue rough on his hand now, as he lay on the bed ready for sleep. He was counting over all the dogs' names he knew, trying to find just the right one, when his eyes finally closed.

He came in from school the following day with one thought only in his mind, but when he asked the question he tried to make it sound as off-hand as possible. "Any mail today, Edna?"

"Only bills." Edna indicated them on the counter. "I'm sure your father won't mind if you pay them."

"I don't get that much allowance, Edna, and you know it."

"You get more than I did when I was your age. I was lucky to have a nickel to spend at the candy store." Edna dampened two shirts and rolled them in a wet tea-towel. "But on the farm I think we had lots of things that you kids don't nowadays."

Kip said, "Did you have a dog, Edna?"

"My goodness, yes. Two of them. Tandy and Gyp."

"Tandy." Kip sounded the word slowly. "I like that name. I'll call my dog that." He had said it aloud before he realized what he was doing. "I mean if I had a dog I'd like to call him that," he hastily corrected himself.

"That's not very likely, is it, with the way your father feels about animals in the house?"

"Maybe, you never can tell." She doesn't know what the letter is going to say, he thought. Just wait until the letter comes.

He did not have long to wait. There was a long envelope on the counter when he came in for lunch the next day. The mail-man had come early. He did not mention it to Edna, and his mother was out with a friend, so that he had to be content with a furtive examination of the postmark. It read Bloom-field. He remembered the name clearly. His father had spoken of it in connection with sand dunes. It sounded like a small country village, the very place where a litter of soft wriggly puppies might be found. His eyes strayed continually to the envelope all through lunch while he tried to show some interest in Edna's conversation.

When Mr. Brooks came in he opened the letter at once, and then called his wife into the living-room. Kip was reluctantly gathering up the dinner silver to set the table for Edna. "Do I really have to do this?" he asked. "There's something I want to get from the bookcase."

"Your father says you have to," Edna said. "Better not complain right now. He's busy with your mother."

He could hear the rustle of the letter, a happy bubble of laughter from his mother and then her voice saying, "He'll be pleased, don't you think, Allan?" He was sure then that it must be a puppy. In his excitement he let a fork clatter to the floor.

Edna looked in on him. "That's one for the kitchen sink, and if you're not more careful with the heirloom silver, we'll have to hire another butler."

"Kip!" His father called from the living-room. "Will you come in here for a minute?"

Kip glanced at Edna, dropped the silver on the table and hurried to his father. "Yes, Dad?" He tried to sound casual.

"Your mother and I have some news we thought you might like to hear."

"It's come through all right as we hoped, dear," Mrs. Brooks put in. "The place is ours."

"The place?" Kip said.

"A place for a new summer cottage," his father said, "down on the Bay of Quinte near Bloomfield."

"Oh?" Kip could not yet understand what they were talking about. He was so sure it had been a dog. "Who is it for?"

"Why, for us, of course, Kip!" Mrs. Brooks laughed. "You'll love it down there!"

"For us?" Kip looked astonished. "But how are we going to find time to spend down there when we have the place up north?"

"We're selling that, Kip," Mr. Brooks explained. "For a long time now we've felt it's too much of a trip for your mother away up there, and living out here makes it even more so. We won't have any trouble getting rid of it. Ted Rogers is interested in buying."

Selling the old cottage? Getting rid of it? Kip could not believe it. Why, they had been going to the lake ever since he could remember, and this year especially he was eagerly looking forward to the end of school so that they could be packed and away, with John and Peter waiting for him in the cottages adjoining. At least if he had no friends here in this new place, he could count on John and Peter, and now they were to be taken away. First of all no dog, and now this! He turned to his father in a sudden burst of anger. "Well, I'm not going!" he shouted. "You can go to the crazy place and I'll stay here!"

"Kip!" Mr. Brooks rose and looked down on him. "What's got into you?"

Mrs. Brooks stared at him, bewildered. "We thought you'd love the whole idea, Kip," she said. "Wait till you see the building we've bought. That's all part of the surprise. And there are all sorts of wonderful places to explore, coves and bays and inlets, and we even passed an Indian Reservation on the way!"

"Who cares about all those things if there's nobody to have fun with? I just hate it here and I'll hate it just as much there. You can have your old place! I don't care if I never see it!" Kip plunged out of the room and down the hall. He slammed his bedroom door behind him and flung himself on his bed. *And to think he had dreamed of a dog!* His cheeks grew hot as he hid his face in the pillow. How thankful he was that he had not made a great fool of himself by mentioning his hopes, when really the letter had nothing to do with him at all. But anger boiled inside him when he thought of it. Making him move to this place where there was nothing to do and nobody to do it with. Buying a new cottage without first asking him if he would like to move from the old one. He knew that had been his father's doing. If his mother had had her way, he would have been in on it from the start, and he could have raised such a fuss then that the whole matter would have been dropped. But it was the thought of the dog that hurt most of all. He had hoped so much that this time his wish would come true. His eyes burned and he dug at the tears with his knuckles. He would not give them the satisfaction of seeing his face wet when his mother brought his dinner in to him.

He sat up slowly, hearing the clatter of cutlery at the table. He was hungry and he would eat his dinner alone in here, leaving them uneasy at his outburst. He wished his mother would hurry. She had never been this long before. He walked to the window and looked out. The spring twilight edged the cedars and towering elms in the valley with apple green. He stared into the darkness at the border of the bush. He was sure he had seen something move into the trees. Perhaps it was a fox. His father had said there might be foxes down there. He went back to sit on the bed and looked at his watch. Half-past six. He knew then with certainty that his mother would not come. The fragrance of roast beef drifted in to the bedroom and made his mouth water. He was starving, but if he wanted something to eat, he would have to go out and face them. Well, he would go hungry. He would not give them the satisfaction of staring at his discomfort. Flinging himself across the bed again, he plugged his ears with his fingers so that he could not hear the sounds from the table. He was furious at their going about the normal business of living as if his disappointments did not matter. It had never happened before.

When he opened his eyes the room was in total darkness. He sat up with a start, blinking. He must have fallen asleep. The house was quite still and he could hear a dog barking across the valley. He felt a vague sense of distaste as he recalled the events of the evening. Stumbling against the maple chest, he made his way to the door and peered out. There were no lights on in the house. He tiptoed to the kitchen and opened the refrigerator door. When he turned, with the bread and cheese in his hands, he let the door slam shut. Edna was sitting at the table in the darkness, her dressing-gown wrapped tightly around her.

"Well?" she said in a low voice.

"I'm hungry," Kip said awkwardly.

"I'd say there isn't any wonder about that," Edna said. "What I want to know is, aren't you proud of yourself?"

Kip said nothing.

"Your mother was in tears before she went to bed, and your father in such a state that he went out and walked till ten-thirty. Now do tell me, young man, how do you feel?"

The bread and cheese tasted dry in Kip's mouth and he pushed it aside. The way Edna stared at him across the table made him feel uncomfortable. "Well," he began belligerently, "they don't have to take everything good away from me, do they?"

"I hadn't noticed that they were trying," Edna said.

"It wouldn't have been so bad if I hadn't thought it was a dog." The tears welled up again and he felt so foolish that he hid his face in his hands. He didn't really care that he had told Edna. She would have found it out anyway, somehow. She always found out everything.

"A dog?" Edna rose slowly and came round to him. "What do you mean?"

"I thought they'd ordered a puppy for me down at that place Bloomfield. I had it all figured out that they were waiting to see how many were in the litter so they could be sure there'd be one for me."

"Oh." Edna sat down beside him. "Now I begin to see a few things. But you're still not excused. And I'd like to know what you're going to do about it."

"What are they going to do about it, you mean," Kip said sullenly.

"No, that *isn't* what I mean," Edna said. "Just because you've always got your own way, doesn't mean you're going to get it this time. And if you ask me, you're going to be doing yourself out of a lot of fun if you don't smarten up."

"What fun could there be down there? It's John and Peter I want, not some new place where I have to start all over again."

"Not even with the Indians?"

"Indians?" Kip turned to her.

"Yes, didn't you hear your mother say there was an Indian Reservation close by?"

"She did say that, didn't she?" In his anger, the words had slipped past Kip almost unnoticed. "I've never known any real Indians."

"Neither have I, but there's no time like the present to start." Edna grinned at him in the darkness. "But *you'll* have to make the start this time."

Kip began to eat again, slowly. "Are they going to take me down there?"

"Your enthusiasm wasn't exactly overwhelming, or do you remember?" Edna said.

"I'll probably hate the place, anyway. Maybe I won't go."

"Maybe you won't get asked again."

Kip straightened. "Don't you think they'll take me now I've made a fuss?"

"I don't know."

"But I couldn't stay here by myself."

"You seemed to think you could. Perhaps they'll leave you here all summer while they're away having a wonderful time with the coves and bays and inlets." She paused. "And with the Indians."

A needle of curiosity began to prick his interest. Coves and bays and inlets. Indians. They sounded like the makings of a wonderful summer and he could have thrown it all away with his own stupidity. Certainly it would be possible for his parents to leave him here for the summer with Edna. He knew that his father must be very angry with him to have forbidden his mother to bring him dinner.

"I don't know what to do," he said slowly.

"You'll find out," Edna said, "and think of that the next time, will you?"

He flung his arm impetuously round Edna's plump shoulders. "Edna, will you ask them for me? If I can go down for the week-end, I mean?"

"Certainly not." Edna rose and moved off towards her bedroom. "That's something between you and your parents, and I suggest you settle it as soon as possible. Goodnight, skipper!"

Kip did not answer. He sat in the darkness of the kitchen searching for a way out. There seemed to be only one, an apology. How could he bring himself to make one? But it did mean a week-end away, and perhaps an entire summer. He looked up with a start at the rustle in the doorway. His father stood there, dimly outlined in the glow from the distant street lamps. Kip rose awkwardly and went towards him. He held out his hand. "I'm sorry, Dad," he said. "I didn't know . . ." He did not know what else to say.

Kip could see the surprise on his father's face as he took the proffered hand and leaned towards Kip in the darkness. "We're going down next week-end; do you want to come?"

"You bet I do," Kip said. It was over. He could have the week-end after all. And there were no reprimands. He was lucky.

"We'll talk about it all in the morning." Mr. Brooks gave him a quick warm pat on the shoulder. "Don't wake your mother. She's just gone off to sleep."

"Okay, I won't." Kip did not know why he suddenly felt so much better. Only the thought of the dog brought him a pang of real regret as he stood looking out into the night-shadowed valley, and far off, beyond the trees, the other dog began to bark again.

2. An Indian Boy and Kip's Cove

The car skimmed along the highway, unfamiliar scenes on every side. "How far now?" Kip asked.

"Not too far," his father said, "but I thought we'd do a little exploring on the way."

"Oh, do we have to?" Kip said.

His mother turned and smiled. "For someone who wasn't going to be at all interested in this place, you're very impatient," she said.

"Well, if we're going we might as well get there," Kip replied. It was true that he could scarcely wait now to see the site of the new cottage, but he would not have said so for the world.

"We can explore some other day, Allan," Mrs. Brooks suggested. "If he wants to go right to West Lake, let's go."

Kip's father gave a nod and said nothing. Kip suddenly wished that he had not spoken. Somehow his father had been so much more approachable this past week, and he wished to do nothing to spoil it.

"There's the Indian Reserve!" Mrs. Brooks called out. "Do you see the sign on the highway? Tyendinaga!"

Kip rolled down the window and took in the scene with one disappointed glance. "But there are only houses and fields," he said.

"What did you expect? Wigwams and longhouses?" Kip could hear the quiet chuckle in his father's voice. "But then I mustn't forget, you've never seen an Indian Reserve before now, have you, Kip?"

"No, but I didn't think it would be just like everywhere else." Kip watched three small dark-skinned boys playing in a large pond made by the spring rains. They looked no different from him.

"There's no reason why it shouldn't be," his father said. "Indians live and work as we do now, except that they live together on special tracts of land set aside for them."

"Tyendinaga," Mrs. Brooks said. "I wonder what that word means."

Kip wondered, too. Perhaps there would be a book in which he could look it up. He loved to read and he visited the library at least once a week. The next time he would ask the librarian for a book of Indian words. "Anyway," he said happily, "if that's the Reserve, it won't be long now."

"Don't get your hopes too high, Kip," Mr. Brooks put in. "It's nearly two hours' drive yet."

"Two hours!" Kip straightened in his seat. "But I thought you said the Indians were close by the cottage!"

His mother looked worried at his obvious disappointment. "No, I said that we had passed a Reserve on the way, dear," she explained. "You must have misunderstood."

Kip sank back in the corner. So that was that. He had counted on the Indians and they could not be included in the picture at all. He now wondered sullenly if this new place would have anything he liked. But he could not be gloomy for long. It was a beautiful spring day, with the fresh buds misting the winter skeletons of the trees with green, and water glinting on every side. He caught a swift glimpse of a wide river and two boys, older than the others but Indians like them, poling their way on its placid surface on a rudely constructed raft. "Like Huckleberry Finn," he thought. "They've made it themselves and they're going on an adventure." He wondered if they had their lunches with them and would anchor their craft far upstream to build a roaring camp-fire for their meal. Perhaps they would even sleep out under the stars. That happened all the time in books. Sometimes it happened to real boys, too. Mike had gone on a camping trip with his cub pack to Algonquin Park, and they had lived outdoors for a whole week. One night they had awakened to find a bear in camp. He pictured the camp-fire smouldering in the darkness, the boys in their bags sleeping in the wilderness and the lumbering tread of the bear as he crashed in upon the scene. He shivered with the joy of it. If only his mother would let him go away to camp. But she never would. She said you never knew what might happen in those places so far away from home.

"Why so quiet, Kip?" His mother turned to look at him. "Aren't you enjoying the drive?"

"Sure." They would never know what he was thinking. That was the wonderful thing about thoughts. They were all your own.

"We'll soon be in Napanee," she said. "We'll stop there for lunch."

Kip brightened at the prospect of food. He loved to eat out, even if Edna was a marvellous cook. He wished she could have come with them, but she had gone to visit her sister for the week-end.

"That looks like a nice place, Allan." They had entered the town of Napanee and his mother was eyeing a trim frame restaurant with cheerful red awnings. "Let's stop here."

"I'm starved," Kip said.

His father gave him a playful cuff on the shoulder as they

walked away from the car. "Where have I heard that before?" he said.

They were on their way again within an hour. "We'll go down and take the ferry at Adolphustown," Mr. Brooks said. "There's some beautiful country through here." Even as he spoke the rolling farm land was becoming more abundant with meadow grasses and spring planting.

"Dad, wait!" Kip poked his head out of the window.

The car braked to a lurching stop round a bend in the highway. "Whatever is the matter?" Mrs. Brooks looked back in alarm. "Did you see something on the highway?"

"No, there's a sign back there at the side road we just passed," Kip said. "It says something about a church and there was a date underneath, seventeen something."

"Oh?" His father gave him a quizzical glance. "Let's go back and find out what it's all about."

Wind and rain had blurred the outlines of the lettering on the sign but it was still legible. "Hay Bay Church," Kip read aloud. "Seventeen ninety-two." He gazed up at his father. "Zowie! That was an awful long time ago!"

"It was, wasn't it?" Mr. Brooks said. "Shall we go?"

"Let's!" Kip bounded back into the car. "Do you think it'll be just like it was then, away back in seventeen ninety-two, I mean?"

"We'll have to wait to find that out," his mother said. "We told you there were plenty of interesting spots around here, didn't we?"

Mr. Brooks steered the car on to the unfamiliar country road, but he found it impossible to hurry. The way was rutted from the spring rains and wound unexpectedly through rows of maples and beech. Muddy farm lanes came into view with sometimes a dog leaping out to bark at their wheels, sometimes a group of silent children staring from a wooden farm gate.

"There! That's Hay Bay, Kip!" Mrs. Brooks said. A wide

vista of water rippled in the May sunshine. Long jetties of land, dotted with groves of red cedars, pierced the water like enormous needles knitting together the wide ribbon of hay that bound the shores. The fields on both sides of the water were brilliant green with the coming summer and starred with dandelions.

"Were we right when we thought the sign was pointing this way?" Mr. Brooks brought the car to a stop. "We've come down here for miles and not another sign in sight, to say nothing of a church."

"Perhaps we'd better turn back," Mrs. Brooks said. "This road is almost impassable in spots."

"Wait a minute, Dad!" Kip sang out. "There's a boy over there beside the barn. Can I get out and ask him?"

"Help yourself!" Mr. Brooks leaned back and lit his pipe. "And don't get into any discussion about the price of crops."

Kip grinned. "That's not very likely. That's something I don't know anything about."

The boy must have been about sixteen. He was tall and strong, heaving large fork-loads of manure from a heap beside the barn to a trailer behind the farm tractor. He looked up with a start when Kip called. "Good day," he said politely. "Can I help you?"

Kip eyed him before he spoke, wishing he could have a boy like that for a friend. "We're looking for Hay Bay Church, the one on the sign at the highway," he said.

"You've come to the right place," the boy said. "It's only another mile down the road, but we keep the key here. Come on up and I'll get it for you."

Kip climbed the fence and followed the boy to the red brick farmhouse that stood in a grove of maples well back from the road. The delicious fragrance of spiced cookies met them at the door.

"Someone for the church key, Mother!" the boy called as they went in.

"Good! You're one of the first this spring." The boy's mother brushed her hair from her hot forehead with a floury hand and reached for a book on a nearby shelf. "You must sign the visitors' book. Have a cookie while I fetch Dad's old pen. It's never here when I want it."

Self-consciously Kip took a cookie from the plate the boy offered him. There was silence between them but it was companionable. The big farm kitchen reminded him of Edna and the one at her old farm home about which she had so often told him. It was low-ceilinged and spacious with an old-fashioned woodstove in one corner and red geraniums crowding the window-sills.

"Sorry to be so long." The farmer's wife re-entered the room and handed him the pen. "Sign here, will you, please?"

Kip read the names on the open page in surprise. "Visitors from the States come here, too?"

"Some of them can trace their relations away back to the first settlers who built Hay Bay Church," the woman said. "That's one of the reasons they come here."

He wondered, as he thanked them and made off for the car, if the farm boy would look in the book to see what his name was. He wished very much that he could have him for a friend. He was older and could doubtless teach him a great many things. He opened the car door with a rush. "Guess what!" he exclaimed. "I signed the visitors' book, and there are all kinds of names in there from the States. People come all that way to see this church. It must be really something!"

"The first pioneers to settle this area came from the United States," his father said as he started the car. "They came here by the hundreds during the revolutionary war against England so that they could go on living under the British flag. You must have studied about them at school."

"I guess we did," Kip admitted, "but it didn't seem real like this."

"There's a sign!" Mrs. Brooks sang out. "It said National Historic Site."

"We're nearly there!" Mr. Brooks swung the car round a sharp curve and the church, a dark-brown, square frame building, stood before them on a willow-lined cove of the bay.

Kip stared at it. "But it just looks like an old barn!" he said. He could not keep the disappointment from his voice.

"It is like a barn, Kip," his father said. "But remember every bit of it was put up by hand in hours stolen from clearing the wilderness and tending crops. Look, there's a sign on the lawn. Read it for us, Kip."

Kip was impatient to go inside the church, but he moved towards the sign on the well-kept lawn and began to read. "Hay Bay Church, 1792. In 1791, William Losee, an itinerant preacher . . ." he paused. "What does that mean?"

"That's a minister who goes preaching from place to place about the countryside. Some of them would cover hundreds of miles." Mrs. Brooks spread the car rug on the lawn and sat down in the warm sunlight.

". . . organized in this district the first Methodist circuit in Upper Canada. This meeting house, Upper Canada's first Methodist Chapel, was built in 1792." Kip eyed the church curiously. It seemed astonishing to think that people had been passing in and out of those rough-hewn doors for over a hundred and fifty years. He read the rest of the words in a rush and turned to his father. "Can we go in now, Dad?"

"If this is the right key we can!" Mr. Brooks opened the door and they stepped inside. The windows were heavily shuttered and it took Kip a moment to adjust to the darkness. The dust rose as they moved across the floor, shining in the long ribbons of sunlight that filtered through the shutter cracks. The unvarnished pews were narrow and the beams that supported the ceiling dark-stained and massive. Before them a pulpit of extraordinary height dominated the church, with the old organ well below it. As Kip's eyes followed the pulpit line to its top he became aware of galleries on both sides, high above the pews and overlooking them.

His father saw the question in his eyes. "They really sat up there under the roof, Kip," he said. "As the community grew they made use of all possible space. There wasn't much time for building new churches in those days."

"I noticed a large stone across the road, Allan," Mrs. Brooks said. "Shall we go over and read what it says?"

Kip spoke quickly. "Can I stay here for a minute?" He was glad when they were gone. This was a secret place and it was wonderful to be alone in it, all the figures from the past crowding round him. He climbed the winding staircase to the left gallery and looked about him. Except for the muted twittering of the sparrows in the eaves, the little church was full of the silence of days long ago. Kip would not have been surprised, in the quiet, to see a stalwart pioneer in hobnail boots and homespun come striding up the aisle. Then he caught sight of a typewritten paper tacked to the wall. He read it, forgetting the time and his parents. It told of the flight of the refugees from the revolutionary war in the United States, of their journey to Upper Canada, five ship-loads of them, families of wealth and property across the border, but here in this new land pioneers in the virgin forest. Each family had been allotted two hundred acres, some seed grain and a cow to share with others, and until the land was divided, they were forced to live in tents in Adolphustown. Adolphustown! The name brought his parents and the present back to mind, and he bounded down the steps and out of the door.

He was surprised to find both his father and the car gone. His mother was once again seated on the car rug, lifting her face to the sun. Her eyes were closed and she had a half smile on her face. She had evidently left her headaches at home. He touched her on the arm gently. "Are you having a sunbath, Mom?"

She opened her eyes. "Oh, I love it here, Kip," she said. "There doesn't seem to be anything to worry about, does there? It's all so quiet and peaceful."

"She could be really pretty if she smiled like that all the

time," Kip thought. And then he remembered all the days she had not been well. Perhaps there was something in what his father said about her needing a change. "Where's Dad gone?" he asked.

"He's taken the key back to save us a little time, dear," she said. "Here he comes now." She rose. "That stone memorial across the road is for Paul and Solomon Huff," she added. "They were the first pioneers to settle here and it was Paul who donated the land for the church."

"Everybody ready for Adolphustown?" Mr. Brooks called from the car. "The farm folks told me the way."

They were on it in a moment, passing a large stone cairn erected to honour Sir John A. Macdonald, and an old pioneer cemetery where the flat markers, pitted with weather, were scarcely visible for wild roses and hawthorn trees. They were in Adolphustown in half an hour, standing beside the oldest church bell in Canada, cracked and green with age.

"Boy!" Kip said. "This thing was made in Bristol, England, in 1690. Imagine anything being that old!" He realized that boys like himself must have listened to it pealing long years ago. He wondered what games they played and if they had to go to school in the wilderness.

"Let's have an ice-cream cone," Mr. Brooks suggested as they drove through the small village. "It isn't everyone can buy a cone at one of the oldest stores in Upper Canada." They all gazed at the sign which declared the white frame building a United Empire Loyalist trading-post built in 1819. "The storekeeper tells me the actual landing spot of the pioneers is down that way near the memorial," he said as he came out with the ice-cream.

They drove down to the great stone shaft standing where the tents of the pioneers were first pitched in 1784, and then on a few miles to the car ferry which carried them over the water to Glenora.

Mr. Brooks slowed the car as they came round a curve and

approached a steep road, leaving the highway on the left. "Shall we go up to see the Lake on the Mountain?" he asked.

"Oh, no, not this trip, Allan," Mrs. Brooks said. "Please, do let's find a place to stay first." Kip could hear tiredness in her voice.

"I've heard there's a strange cave up there in the side of the mountain," Mr. Brooks said. "I thought Kip might like to see it. But we'll come back some other time. We'll go on to Picton now to find a motel, and then on to the Sandbanks."

When the arrangements for the night had been made, they drove on to Bloomfield, a pleasant little village, its streets lined with chestnuts and maples. Kip was surprised when his father stopped before the general store.

"Kip, will you run in, please, and ask the storekeeper for the key he's keeping for me? His name is Mr. Bell."

"The key? What for?" Kip asked.

"You'll find out," his mother smiled.

Kip wondered as he climbed out of the car and up the wide verandah steps. If there was a key a cottage must already stand on the West Lake site. The prospect of a big new summer home excited him. If it were large enough he could invite Mike and Brian up here to spend some of the summer with him. Then there would be no worry about someone to have fun with. He opened the screen door and walked in, and nearly bumped into a fly paper dangling from the ceiling.

"Hello." Mr. Bell's face was genial. "What can we do for you today?"

"I'm Christopher Brooks," Kip said. "My father sent me in to ask for the key."

"Well, it's nice to meet you, Chris." Mr. Bell extended his hand across the well-worn counter. "So you're the fellow who's going to go to school all summer, are you?"

"I think you have me mixed up with somebody else," Kip said rather shyly. "My father has some new property on West Lake."

"No danger of me getting mixed up," Mr. Bell laughed. "I've been around these parts for over fifty years, eh, Dan?"

Kip heard a chuckle and turned to see a tall slim figure sitting on an orange crate near the window, a dog at his feet. "He's like the farm boy but maybe not as old," Kip thought, "but his hair is really dark and he's so tanned."

"Anyway, here's the key, and good luck!" Mr. Bell handed it to him. "All the pioneers of Bloomfield will be waiting down there with their pencils and slates to meet you. Ghosts, of course!" he added with another laugh.

"Ghosts!" thought Kip. "What can he be talking about?" Aloud he said, "Thank you very much, Mr. Bell," stealing another glance at the boy as he went out.

"How did you like Mr. Bell?" His mother had the car door open for him.

Kip smiled. "He's all right, I guess, but he sure had me mixed up with somebody else."

"Oh?" His father sounded puzzled. "What do you mean by that?"

"He said something about me going to school all summer and then he was talking about the old pioneers, ghosts or something like that." Kip did not see the quick exchange of glances between his parents. "There was a boy in there," he added eagerly. "He sure had a good tan, and he had a dog, too."

"A good tan?" Mr. Brooks steered the car down the narrow highway past a canning factory, over a bubbling creek shaded by huge trees, and on through farm land crowned with dense hardwood bushes.

"Are you sure he wasn't an Indian?" his mother asked.

"An Indian!" The idea had not occurred to him. Excitement rose in him at the thought. "I've never seen an Indian, so I don't know."

"Dark skin and eyes, high cheek-bones, dark hair," his father said. "Does that sound like him?"

"Exactly," Kip agreed. "And he has a dog! Lucky thing!"

"Indians love dogs," Mrs. Brooks said. "But why would the boy be so far away up here?"

"It isn't that far really," Kip's father said. "There's a ferry near Deseronto that would bring him down here on a shorter route. His father is probably doing work on the cottages for some of the summer visitors."

Kip had no more time to speculate about the boy. His father sang out suddenly, "Let's pull in here and find out what's at the end of this muddy lane!" And he knew they had arrived.

Their feet were clogged with mud by the time they reached the tree line. Kip plunged on ahead and broke through the trees to the sound of water crashing on the shore. It was a small cove ringed round with clumps of tall cedars. West Lake stretched before him, the waves frosted with white as a strong wind buffeted the water. He looked to the southwest and held his breath. Hills of gleaming hard white sand rose in the distance, slopes and dunes scattered sparsely with trees and shrubs. His father came up beside him. "The Sandbanks," he said briefly.

"What's on the other side?" Kip asked.

"Lake Ontario. It's the arm of the Sandbanks reaching out that makes West Lake here."

"It's beautiful," his mother said. "We couldn't have found a better spot."

But Kip was already following a little path uphill through the cedars. He stopped short as he reached the crest of the slope and the building sprang into view. It was a large log structure weathered to a grey-brown that blended perfectly with the woodland surroundings. The shutters were loose and banging noisily in the wind, the chinks between the logs crumbling, but the cabin stood firm, its shoulders broad to the gales like a stalwart pioneer.

"It's like a school!" Kip shouted.

"It is a school," his father called behind him. "A school

nobody wants because it's had its day. So we bought it for ourselves. How do you like it?"

"It's a funny-looking place all right," Kip said, "but where's the summer cottage?"

Mrs. Brooks came through the trees. "Why, this is it, dear," she laughed. "We're going to make it exactly the way we want it. Isn't that exciting?"

Exciting! Kip's heart sank as he gazed around him. An old pioneer school, and he had dreamed of a huge sprawling summer home with enough rooms left over for Mike and Brian. Why, they would never finish this place in one summer! How could they come and stay here, even over a week-end?

"It won't take us long to get it into trim." Mr. Brooks was inspecting the ancient rain barrel at the back of the cabin. "We'll find a handyman in the village who can do the job and we'll be in it in no time."

"Who cares?" thought Kip. "It's not even big enough for us, let alone Mike and Brian." But he did not say so. He had already been in quite enough trouble the last time. He remembered now the words Mr. Bell had spoken. "Dad," he said suddenly, "there wouldn't really be ghosts here, would there?"

"Oh, you never can tell." Kip did not know just how seriously to take the half bantering tone. "After all this place has stood here for over a hundred years. Some of the old students might want to come back to visit the scene of their crimes."

Mrs. Brooks laughed. "Don't scare him, Allan. He's only fooling, dear. Don't you go worrying about ghosts."

"Oh, I'm not worrying," Kip said. But as he spoke he shivered, half in fear, and half in delight.

"Let's go in." Mr. Brooks put the key in the battered door and it opened with a whining of hinges.

It took a moment for Kip's eyes to adjust to the darkness. "Dad, the blackboard's still here," he said, "and all the desks."

Mrs. Brooks passed her hand over one of them. "The teacher hasn't been doing her dusting lately," she said.

Kip and his father laughed. "I wonder how I'd feel in one of these," Kip said. He sat down at the old-fashioned desk while his mother eyed him with horror.

"Kip, your pants!" she cried. "You'll have them covered with all the dust of a hundred years!"

"Not quite that long, Bet," Mr. Brooks said. "The school was used off and on up until ten years ago. So Mr. Bell told me." He leaned against the blackboard and puffed on his pipe. "Well, Kip," he said, "how do you like it?"

"It's—it's quite a place," Kip said. He did not know what else to say. He was unwilling to show the enthusiasm his parents obviously expected of him. Still, he could not deny that the old cabin had a certain fascination. When he thought about it, it was like the old church at Hay Bay, and here as there, the pioneers had walked and learned and sung, and danced in their calico and homespun. If only there had been a cottage close by with room for Mike and Brian!

They locked the door and walked down to the edge of the hill where wind-tossed West Lake came into view, the spume flying like flocks of sea-birds skipping the waves.

Kip's eyes followed the line of the tree-crowded shore, searching. "Isn't there even one cottage around here?" he asked finally.

His mother was standing quite still, gazing with complete satisfaction at the panorama of wind and wave and sand-banks. "No, Kip," she said happily. "We're going to be very quiet and alone. There's only a lodge and it's much farther up the shore."

"There seem to be a few cottages up there in that cove on the north shore," Mr. Brooks said.

"Yes, and a lot of good that will do me," Kip thought. "Not one single person to have any fun with." And yet as the wind rocked the cedars and the waves boomed on the shore, something stirred his blood. It was certainly the kind of place where things could happen. "Does this place have a name?" he asked.

"You mean this cove?" His father shook his head. "Not that we know of, but it should have, shouldn't it?"

"Kip's Cove," Mrs. Brooks said. "How do you like the sound of that?" She smiled affectionately at her son. "Kip's Cove."

Mr. Brooks looked pleased. "I like it, but the question is, does the young man like the spot well enough to have it named after him?" He gazed shrewdly at Kip.

"Oh, I like it, Dad!" The thought of having a place with his name on it pleased him enormously. Maybe one day someone would draw a map of West Lake with all the little bays and inlets and there his name would be, printed for everyone to see – *Kip's Cove*. Suddenly he remembered the Indian boy and the whole prospect grew brighter. Perhaps he would meet him again. "Dad," he said, "do we have to take the key back to the store?"

"I think it's wise to leave it there," Mr. Brooks said. He began to descend the hill. "Shall we go now?"

The village street was deserted as they drove up to the store. "I'll take the key in, Dad," Kip said quickly. "Don't you bother getting out."

"I really should go in and ask Mr. Bell about village carpenters," Mr. Brooks said. Then he glanced at Kip. "Well, maybe I'll wait and take a trip up next week-end. Run along then."

Kip's heart sank as he opened the screen door. There was no one in the store at all. The Indian boy had gone. Mr. Bell came from his living-quarters behind the shelves of groceries. "So now you have a school all to yourself," he beamed. "How do you like it?"

"It's fine, thank you." Kip wondered if he dared ask him where the boy lived, and then thought better of it. Perhaps Mr. Bell would think him queer.

"Well, you're camped right on an Indian trail," Mr. Bell was saying. "Don't be surprised if you hear a few war-whoops in the dark of a moonless night." He winked at Kip.

Kip leaned across the counter. "How do you mean?"

"Just what I said," Mr. Bell smiled. "There was a cross-country Indian route right about where your old school stands now. Did you find the creek?"

"Creek?" Kip said. "No, we never saw any creek."

"It's down the little slope to the north of the school. Kids used to have a whale of a time fishing in it at noon hour when the place was in use." Mr. Bell reached up to a nearby shelf. "Here. You take along a candy bar to chew on the way home."

"Thanks a lot," Kip said. He longed to ask him more about the Indians and the trail, but he knew his father was waiting. "Thanks," he said again. "See you soon!"

"I hope so!" Mr. Bell called. "Let us know if we can do anything for you!"

Kip saw the Indian boy as soon as he opened the door. He was coming up the narrow rutted lane that ran beside the store to the sheds in the rear. He was whistling to his dog who had stopped to sniff at a pile of cartons beside the fence. Kip really did not know later what made him act so quickly. He saw the boy and he knew that he wanted the boy to see him. And he had always been an excellent jumper at school, three times winner at the annual field day. With one bound he leaped down the verandah steps, intending to land on both feet on the broken cement sidewalk at the bottom. But in a moment he lay sprawled on the ground. His heel had caught in the shoe-scraper on the bottom step, and there he was prone, his legs reaching into the mud of the lane. He lifted his eyes shamefacedly to find the boy standing over him. Suddenly he felt something wet and cold on his cheek. It was the boy's dog.

"Away, Tad! Away!" The Indian lad pulled the dog back.

"It's all right." Kip was thankful for the dog. It took attention for the moment from his foolish predicament.

"Say, are you hurt?" The boy gazed at him anxiously.

"Oh, no, I'm not hurt at all." Kip's left knee was stinging

and his elbows were sore but he would not have admitted it for the world. He glanced at the car. His parents were deep in conversation. They had not seen his mishap at all. He put his arms round the dog who continued to lick his face. "He's a good old thing."

"Not so old," the boy said. "Just seven months. That's why he still acts like a puppy." He watched Kip as he stood up with effort. "Are you sure you're all right?"

"Sure, I'm okay." He did not know what else to say, and his father had turned to look at them. "Well," he added lamely, "I guess I'd better get going."

"Good-bye!" The Indian boy whistled to the dog and made off down the street.

Kip's father got out of the car and came towards him. He eyed the dust and mud on his pants and wind-breaker. "What on earth have you been doing?" he asked.

"I fell," Kip said, but he was still staring after the boy. How he wished that he had not made a fool of himself. And at their first real encounter, too. He waited for sharp words from his father but the latter, too, was watching the boy's departure.

"He looks like a nice lad," he said. "Perhaps you'll meet him again."

"Maybe," Kip said, but he did not think it likely. This village was a long, long way from home, and even the pioneer school was not really close to Bloomfield. Besides, it would be weeks before the cottage was finished and he could come with his mother and Edna for a summer holiday.

He scarcely heard his mother's expression of concern when he got into the car and they began to drive off. He was gazing out of the back window, trying to catch a last glimpse of the boy and his dog, watching the village of Bloomfield become a haze of greenery and sunlight far behind them on the highway.

3. A Ghost or Two

"And then we climbed a hill all covered with cedars, and guess what we found at the top!" Kip paused dramatically, his sandwich in mid-air. He was in the kitchen at lunch two days later, describing the week-end trip to Edna who had just arrived on the morning train.

Edna mimicked him, holding the teapot she was carrying high in a melodramatic pose. "A herd of wild elephants!"

"Oh, Edna!" Kip laughed in spite of himself. That was just like Edna. She always had to make a joke out of everything. "How would a herd of wild elephants ever find their way to Ontario?"

"I don't know." Edna shrugged her shoulders. "Maybe they ran away from a circus. That's it. That's what they did! The animal trainer was a cruel man with a long black moustache, and he used to beat them. So one night they decided to make a run for it. Now these elephants . . ."

"Edna!" If his own story, especially the part about the Indian boy, had not been so important, he would have let her ramble on in her usual fashion, because it was so highly entertaining. Together, in this haphazard manner, they had made up dozens of stories.

"Now what have I done wrong?" Edna poured her tea. "I think that one has a wonderful beginning. We could make a super-duper tale out of it."

"Don't you want to hear about the place?" Kip said. "And who we met?"

"Of course I do, love," Edna nodded. "You just go right ahead and tell me. I'm all ears." That was just like Edna, too. Good old Edna! "Well, it was an old log school, a pioneer school!"

"That sounds wonderful!"

"Sure, it would be all right if they didn't want to use it for a summer cottage." Kip wrinkled his nose in distaste. "I don't see how they can ever do it. It'll take months to get it finished."

Edna rose to fetch the lemon pudding. "I wouldn't say that, not if the outside structure is tidy and firm. You'd be surprised how fast you can smack on a bit of carpentry."

"Anyway, Mom said we should call it Kip's Cove and Dad seemed to think it was okay for a name."

"Well, well, sir," Edna said. "You won't want me eating lunch at the same table, not now that you've had a place named after you. I'll go eat on the back porch."

"Oh, Edna, you big old silly." Kip grinned sheepishly. "It's not much of a place, anyway, just a bunch of old logs and a lot of water. But you know what? Mr. Bell said there was an Indian trail past there once! And there was an Indian boy at the store and he spoke to me. His dog jumped up on me and licked me all over my face!" He omitted the part about the leap down the steps and the fall. Edna did not need to know that.

"Was he your age?" Edna was definitely interested.

"Older, I think. He was taller than I am, anyway." Kip smiled, remembering. "He sure had a nice dog."

Edna said nothing for a moment. She rose and began to stack the dirty dishes beside the sink. "What are you doing after school tonight?" she said finally.

"Oh, I thought I might go down to the ravine and see if I could make a fort or something," Kip said. "Edna, do you think it would be very hard to build a tree house? I mean, would you need to know much carpentry?"

"Not for that kind of thing. Just make sure you know where your thumb is." Edna was quiet again. Then, "But it seems to me there are places that could use your carpentry more than a tree house."

"What do you mean?" Kip stared at her, puzzled.

"You figure it out, skipper," Edna smiled. "I'm going to tackle the dishes."

He thought over her words as he rode his bike to school. Then the idea came to him. Edna was thinking of the pioneer school! It could be only that! She was suggesting that he help with the remodelling. But how could he help when he knew so little carpentry, and why should he, anyway, when he didn't really want the old place for a summer cottage in the beginning? But then, if he persuaded his father that they should work on it together, might there not be the chance, on the many week-ends spent there, of meeting the Indian boy again? Once his mind was made up he could not wait for school to be done so that he could be on his way home. Only one problem plagued him while he neglected the map which he should have been drawing. How was he to learn sufficient carpentry to persuade his father that he was good enough to help?

When he clattered in at the back door after school, Edna was nowhere in sight. He raced downstairs.

Edna was sorting clothes for the dryer. "Hi!" she said. "Your mother hasn't come home from down town yet. There's an orange in the 'frig and cookies in the jar if you want to help yourself."

"Edna, I've got an idea," Kip burst out, "but I don't know how to begin."

"At the beginning, that's the proper place," Edna said. She went on shaking out the clothes.

Kip tugged at her arm. "Edna, stop working! I want to talk to you!"

Edna eyed him with lifted eyebrows. "I've told you before, young man," she said, "that I don't like being ordered around. And neither does anyone else. Remember that, and you'll be a lot happier."

"I'm sorry, Edna, but please listen. I've got an idea and you've got to help me with it. I mean I'd like you to help me with it," he hastily corrected himself.

Edna sat down on the step. "That's better. What's up now?"

"Edna, I've got to learn how to do carpentry. How can I do it?"

"My, my! Is the tree house that important?" Edna said.

"Oh, no, it isn't the tree house! It's the old school. I've been thinking it all out. Why couldn't I help Dad with the work up there on week-ends? Think of all the money we'd save, and how happy Dad would be to get some real help!"

"To say nothing of the fact that you might run into that Indian boy and his dog again, if you went up there that often," Edna said.

Kip kicked the bottom step. "Well, there's nothing wrong with that, is there?"

"No," Edna said, "but let's be honest with ourselves, shall we? So you want to learn how to use a hammer and saw. Okay, when do we start?"

"We?" Kip queried.

"Well, I suppose you have to learn from somebody and I think I am as good as the next fellow."

"You mean you can do things with hammers and saws?"

Edna smiled at his astonishment. "I wasn't brought up on a farm for nothing, skipper!"

"Edna, that's super!" Kip gave her an impulsive hug. "Let's get started right now!" He went into his father's small workroom.

Edna followed him. "It's all right today, but we won't be able to do it when your mother's home. She couldn't stand the noise."

"Oh, Edna, don't tell Mom!" Kip looked horrified. "She'd never let me use a saw. She'd think I'd saw my arm off or something!" His mother had an imagination of her own when it came to disasters. "She's out so much with this old bazaar and strawberry tea thing anyway, that we should have lots of time."

"That's true enough," Edna agreed. "Come on then, let's go!"

Kip struggled with the saw under Edna's watchful eye for fifteen minutes, then, with a sudden burst of impatience, he flung it to the floor. "I'll never be able to work the old thing!" he shouted. "I can't even get it started!"

Edna's lips made a tight, firm line. "You do that again, young man, and that's the end of the carpentry lessons. Pick up that saw and get going."

"But it looks so easy!" Kip wailed. He tried again and this time felt the saw bite into the wood. It was only a beginning but it made him feel triumphant.

Edna went upstairs and came back with a plate of cookies and a glass of milk. "Here," she said. "You need some strength. Carpentry is hard work."

Kip sat down on the saw-horse and helped himself to a cookie. The spicy flavour took him back at once to the fragrant farm kitchen on the road to Hay Bay. "Edna," he exclaimed. "I left out part of the story when I was telling you about the week-end. I went to a farmhouse and the kitchen was just like the one where you used to live. It had a big wood-stove and red geraniums."

"Where was all this?" Edna helped herself to a cookie, too.

"On the way to the pioneer school." Edna listened while Kip told her of the church, Adolphustown, and the pioneers.

"I know a little about the Loyalists who came from the States," Edna said. "Some of the very early ones settled near our district at Stirling. As a matter of fact the old house was still standing on the edge of town."

Kip leaned towards her. "What did it look like? Was it all logs?"

"Oh, no. It was a great two-storey affair, all stone, but it was so old some of the stones were crumbling." Edna smiled to herself. "I remember the story that went around about the ghosts."

"Ghosts!" Kip said. "Was it haunted?"

"So they said. The first settler came there away back in seventeen-ninety. From what I'd heard he'd had an adventure with the Indians when he was a boy in the States. And they used to say that on a still night you could hear him calling an Indian name."

Kip shivered. Indians and ghosts all in one story! It was almost too much. "Did you ever go there to find out?" he asked.

"We did. We made up our minds to spend the night there one Hallowe'en, without telling our parents, of course," Edna said. "There were three of us, two boys and myself. I wouldn't let the boys do anything where I couldn't follow." She laughed. "I was too much of a tomboy."

"Edna, go on!" Kip begged. "I mean, *please*. I want to know what happened."

"Well, we all crept out of the house about ten at night. I had to shinny down the drainpipe because my room was on the second floor. I still have the mark of that drainpipe on my ankle," Edna said. "Even the garden of the house was a scary enough place, all overgrown with weeds and rose bushes run wild. We were all scratched and torn by the time we reached the back window. I volunteered to go in first if the boys would boost me up." Edna grinned. "I told you I was a tomboy!"

"Weren't you even scared?" Kip said.

"Sure thing I was, shaking in my shoes, especially when I was waiting in the dark musty room for the boys to follow me. You see, most of the furniture in the room was still there just as it had been years ago, and it looked as if someone could come walking in on us any minute."

"Did they?"

"We never found out. We tiptoed across the living-room to the staircase to explore the second storey. And you know, the funny thing was that there was no dust!"

"No dust?" Kip drew a sharp breath. "But you said the place hadn't been lived in for years!"

"I know, and it hadn't, but there was none. Anyway, we began to climb the stairs, and oh, how they creaked! I was really scared!" Edna's eyes sparkled. "Just when we were on the top step it happened!"

Kip wanted to speak but he could not. He was so charged with excitement and suspense.

"Suddenly beneath us, in what we call a summer kitchen, we heard a little bell ringing loud and clear. And don't ask me what it was because we never waited to find out! We leaped and tumbled down the stairs like wild things, and even fought about getting out of the window. And if there wasn't any dust in that house, believe me, there certainly was on the village road when we were streaking for home."

Kip came to sit beside her on the step. "But that isn't all! You must have found out later what it was all about!"

"Indeed, we didn't!" Edna spoke with emphasis. "We never went near the place again. We didn't even get as close as the cottage next door, and that was a queer one, too."

"Why?"

"There was an old hermit living in there. Well, he was old to me at the time, anyway." Edna smiled sadly. "We can be pretty cruel when we're young, Kip, and I know we gave him a bad time. He never spoke to anyone, just went up to the store once in a while to pick up some groceries, and had to listen to us taunting him on the way back."

Kip felt uncomfortable. He had done things like that sometimes, but suddenly the old man seemed very real to him. "You didn't really hurt him, did you, Edna?"

"Not physically, love, but there are other ways," Edna said. "He wasn't so old as I remember now. Fifty-five maybe. Mind you, he'd be well along now for that was nearly twenty years ago. The last time I heard he was still living there, all alone." She sprang to her feet as they heard a sound at the front door. "My gracious! There's your mother home, and not a bit of dinner on the stove yet."

Kip listened. "It isn't Mom," he said. "It's only the paperboy. And don't forget, Edna. Don't breathe a word about the carpentry. We'll tell them when I know how to do it."

Later, while he lay in bed waiting for sleep to come, he thought of Edna's story again. She had told him so much of her childhood that it was as real to him as if he had lived it himself. He wished that he could go there and see the setting of Edna's adventures. It would be like stepping into the pages of a much-loved story-book. Now especially did he want to go, to see the great stone house where a ghost walked who called an Indian name. He heard the dog barking across the ravine. It had a far-off lonesome sound in the stillness of the night. He drew the covers quickly up to his chin and fell asleep.

In the days that followed Kip was thankful for his mother's plans at the women's club. Since their move the church was far enough away that the coming and going kept her from the house until dinner-time every evening, and sometimes even after that. Two nights his father stayed at the office and they had the house to themselves. He finished his homework in one determined rush and spent an hour and a half in the basement with Edna before bedtime.

"It's just as well you're making progress," Edna remarked on the Thursday night when they came upstairs. "Your mother's nearly finished with her bazaar, and I doubt if she'll be going much more."

"But it isn't till June when the strawberries are ripe," Kip said.

"I know, but your mother isn't going to keep on till then. She said she'd finish up what she promised and then start you all at a church in the district here. St. David's, I suppose. There's really no need for you to go away over there every week, anyway. You'll have to change churches some time."

Kip sawed away with a flourish and a piece of two-by-four fell to the floor. "Well, how am I doing?"

"Fair, I guess," admitted Edna. "But don't get too cocky about it. You still have a lot to learn. Still," she conceded, "you could learn that on the job."

"Do you think I could tell Dad now?" Kip asked eagerly.

"Ask him, don't tell him," Edna advised. "Yes, I think you're ready."

He waited until they were all at the table the following evening. When Edna brought in the lemon pie he spoke up, "Dad," he said, trying to sound off-hand, "when are you going to start to work on the school?"

His father looked pleased at the question. "Why, I thought I'd take a run down this week-end, Kip, and see if I can find someone in the village to give me a hand."

"Why not me?" Kip had planned to broach the subject much more cautiously than that but the words had tumbled out.

"You!" His mother laughed. "We'd end up visiting the hospital instead of Kip's Cove if that were the case!"

"But I know how to use a hammer and saw! Edna's been teaching me every day for hours and hours all week!"

Edna nodded. "It's true, Mr. Brooks. He's not a bad hand at it, either."

"You actually mean you've been *sawing*!" Kip's mother said the last word as if it were a matter of life and death. "But you can't do that, dear! Goodness knows what you're liable to do to yourself!"

"But I can!" Kip flung his spoon down. "Edna's taught me how the right way and I won't hurt myself at all."

"Well, this is an interesting development." Kip sighed with relief when he saw his father's smile. "And you really want to help me at the cottage?"

"Oh, yes!" Already he saw the Indian boy and his dog swinging down the village street and himself there to greet them while he bought supplies for his father at the store.

"But he can't, Allan!" He had not counted on so much opposition from his mother. "He's liable to fall off the roof and break a leg!"

"I won't, Mom! Honestly, I won't! I'll be careful!"

"He's almost twelve, Bet," Mr. Brooks said, "and it's time he took a hand in things. I'm glad he's so willing." He looked more than glad. Kip realized that the smile had not left his face. "I still think that we'd better call in a third party to help. It will make the job go that much faster."

Kip did not mind about that as long as he was to be allowed to join the working party. He had sudden compassion for his mother who had fallen silent. "I won't get hurt, Mom." He laid a hand on her arm. "I'll be really careful."

Edna sniffed. "Just remember not to lose your temper if something goes wrong," she warned. "A rooftop is no place for a tantrum."

When Kip and his father started out for Bloomfield the following Saturday morning very early, Kip felt elated. It was the first time that he and his father had ever been away together alone. He did not know what they would talk about all the long way. They never talked much together about anything.

And yet as the miles flew by there was scarcely a minute's silence. There seemed to be so much to discuss about the plans for the summer place, and so much to tell about the places they passed.

When they stopped briefly at the store in the village to ask Mr. Bell about a carpenter, Kip looked in vain for the Indian boy. He did not feel too disappointed when he saw him nowhere in the store or on the street. After all, there would now be many other opportunities to find him. Very soon they were on their way again, driving slowly along one of the small side streets that ran parallel to the highway.

"That must be the place." Mr. Brooks pointed to a frame cottage at the end of a long hedged path. "Mr. Bell said there was a greenhouse behind it."

The long low building behind the house was already bright with bloom and the panes of glass sparkled in the May sunlight. The little cottage was trim and neat, freshly painted in green and white. Flower beds bordered it, rich with velvety green plants and well-turned loam. A rose vine in early bud trailed across the face of the house.

"Good day."

Kip and his father wheeled in surprise as the curt voice sounded over the hedge. The man must have been working on the other side.

"How do you do. Allan Brooks, sir." Mr. Brooks extended his hand as the owner of the voice rounded the hedge and came into view. He was older than Kip's father and shorter, with a lean athletic body. His head was almost entirely bald, with only a brim of white hair, and his eyebrows strongly arched, giving his face an air of strength.

The man took the proffered hand and shook it firmly. When it was Kip's turn for an introduction he found the grasp hard and brief.

"You want something?" Kip saw that this stranger was not one to waste time.

"Mr. Bell told us your name was Mr. Mosely and that you might be interested in doing some carpentry for us at a summer place," Mr. Brooks explained.

"It's possible," Mr. Mosely said, "if it's work that interests me."

Kip tried to stay out of sight behind his father. He did not know if he would like this man. His manner was so abrupt.

"I think it will," Mr. Brooks said. "We're the people who have just bought the old school down on West Lake, and want to make it over into a cottage."

Mr. Mosely's cold blue eyes took them both in. "They should never have sold that place," he said brusquely. "It should have been taken over by the township and made into an historical site."

"Yes, sir, but as it was, it was only going to ruin," Mr. Brooks said quietly. "We've no intention of changing the main building outside. We'll keep the spirit of the old place as much as possible but we'll need to add a bedroom or two for extra quarters."

"All the old places are going." Mr. Mosely seemed not to notice them. "They're all going and nobody does anything about them. History right on our doorstep and it's all being blotted out by superhighways and summer cottages."

"Look here, let me show you the plans I've drawn up." Mr. Brooks sat down on a rustic bench in the nearby rose arbour and spread a sheet of paper on the small table. "You see, I'd like to add a wide verandah the width of the front and two bedrooms like wings in the rear. All of this would stay the same, with the exception of some repair work to the logs and chinks." He frowned, his expression intent. "What would be wrong with our raising a little stone cairn in front of the cottage, telling about its history, and a little about the surrounding district in the old times? You could do that yourself and have it exactly the way you'd like it."

"Maybe," Mr. Mosely said. "I went to that school myself,

and my father and grandfather before me." His eyes narrowed. He seemed to be looking far away. "There was an Indian trail there in the old days, down beside the creek."

"I'm going to look for that," Kip burst in. "Perhaps there'll be Indian relics there."

Mr. Mosely glanced at him, unsmiling. Then he turned to Mr. Brooks. "You can let me know when you want to start. I'll be ready."

"Would you come down with us now, to look the place over?" Mr. Brooks asked.

"I could." Mr. Mosely followed them to the car.

They arrived at the cove half an hour later. They managed to drive the car up the deeply rutted lane almost to the beach. The day was still and warm, and the water made scarcely a whisper on the sand. As they climbed the hill to the school Kip stopped suddenly on the path. "I hear more water," he said, "bubbling over stones."

"The creek," Mr. Mosely said. "When I was a boy your age, I'd have found that for myself long ago."

Kip ran up and over the hill and through the cedars on the other side. Below him, almost hidden by ferns, was the small creek complaining noisily about its tortuous path through the dense undergrowth to the wide reaches of the lake.

"This is perfect!" he shouted to his father who was watching him from the hill-top. "A little river all to ourselves! We could dam it up and have a pond! Or make a waterfall and a bridge!"

Mr. Mosely had been making a circuit of the schoolhouse. "The ghosts in this place won't want you trifling with the scenery. You'd best leave things as they are."

Kip studied the old man's face. It looked perfectly serious. "Ghosts!" he said. "Are there really ghosts here?" Edna's ghost came suddenly to his mind and the sound of the little bell ringing.

His father laughed. "Wouldn't you like a ghost or two

around the cottage, Kip? It would certainly give us a lively summer."

Kip grinned. "I wouldn't mind. I just wondered if Mr. Mosely meant what he said, that's all. Are there really ghosts here?"

"I wouldn't say there were and I wouldn't say there weren't," Mr. Mosely said. "I've heard a tale or two about this place, and about the Outlet where the treasure is buried. Who's to say what's true?"

Treasure! What could he mean by that? But he had turned away as if the subject were closed.

They went round to the front of the building. "With a view like this," Mr. Brooks said, "I'd like a screened verandah here and the bedrooms at the back where Kip can hear his creek bubbling."

"Kip's Creek," Kip smiled. "That sounds okay, too."

"The name of the creek is Willet's Creek," Mr. Mosely said shortly. "It was named after my great-grandfather."

"Oh, well, we won't change it then," Kip hastened to say. "Would we, Dad?" He could almost see Mr. Mosely leaving the job at once if they did!

"No, of course not," Mr. Brooks agreed. "Let's go inside now and decide on our plan of action there."

There were still some half-worked sums on the blackboard almost erased by dust. The floor and desks were gritty with sand. "Wind storms," Mr. Mosely said. "We'll have to fill in all the chinks or you'll have half the beach in your cottage."

Mr. Brooks turned one of the desks over and examined it. "What shall we do with these?" he asked. "They seem to be in fair condition even yet."

"Don't throw them out, Dad," Kip said quickly.

Mr. Mosely's eyes brightened as he looked at Kip. "They don't make this kind any more. We could build a picnic table with them in the grove of cedars out there."

"Let's do it, Dad!" Kip said. "We could put them round in

a ring and make a flower bed in the middle."

Mr. Mosely was positively beaming. "I'll provide the flowers," he said. "Every place should have flowers." Then he was suddenly all business again and the smile was gone. He busied himself jotting down notes of plans and materials. It was late afternoon before they had finished.

"Can we leave you to order everything necessary from the lumber yard, Mr. Mosely?" Mr. Brooks glanced at his watch. "Kip and I have to look for a motel. I think we'll stay overnight and go back in the morning."

"You can stay with me." Mr. Mosely spoke as if the matter needed no discussion. "I have a spare room."

"He's like the captain of a ship," Kip thought as they drove towards the village. "You wouldn't think of saying no to him." He found out why later as they sat in the rose arbour having supper.

"I sailed the lakes once," Mr. Mosely said. "Captain of a freighter. Forty years on the lakes." His eyes lost some of their hardness. "I'd like to be back there sometimes. The young ones don't know how to work a ship these days."

Kip knew now why the house reminded him of a sailing-vessel, neat and trim. "I'd like to be a sailor," he ventured. "It must be lots of fun."

"There's no fun to it," Mr. Mosely said. "It's hard work and plenty of it. Young folks don't want to work nowadays. They have it too soft."

Kip felt quashed. He said nothing.

"I had an Indian lad come in here last year to help me in the greenhouse," Mr. Mosely went on. "He was a good worker but he hasn't come back this year. Thought there was too much to do, I expect."

Kip sat up straight. "An Indian boy? What was his name?"

"Dan Stonefish. His mother and father both teach on the Reserve. His father comes down during the summer months to do jobs about the cottages and some fishing in the bay."

Mr. Brooks eyed Kip. "Your Indian, Kip?"

"It must be, Dad." Kip felt jubilant. At least he knew the boy's name!

Mr. Mosely fumbled in his sweater pocket. "I'm out of tobacco," he said.

"I'll get some at the store for you, Mr. Mosely." Despite the old man's curtness, Kip felt immensely grateful to him. Besides, if he went to the store, he might see Dan there!

"Pick some up for me, Kip," his father said, "and let this be our treat, Mr. Mosely. What brand do you smoke?"

Kip ran down the path to the street and round the corner to the main road. The huge oak tree that shaded the store front cast shadows so deep in the coming dusk that he could not distinguish any one figure among the several lounging on the verandah bench. Silence fell among them as he mounted the steps.

Inside the store lights had not yet been switched on and tinned goods, overalls and packing-boxes were all half shapes in the darkness. He turned to find the tobacco shelf when he saw the large dark brown eyes fixed upon him. The Indian boy was sitting on a tall stool by the window, reading a magazine by the pale half-light. He grinned quickly at Kip. "Hi again!" he said.

"Hi!" Kip said. He could think of nothing more and there was no sign of the dog to keep the conversation flowing.

Mr. Bell came from his living-quarters behind the store. He greeted Kip cheerfully. "So you've come again! How're things going?"

"Just fine thank you, Mr. Bell," Kip said. "We're staying with Mr. Mosely overnight. I'm Christopher Brooks, you know. Remember me?" It was quite obvious that Mr. Bell remembered him. Kip said the name only for the Indian boy's benefit.

"Of course I do. You're the folks who've bought the old school." Mr. Bell leaned his plump elbows on the counter.

"How are things making out down there?"

"Mr. Mosely was down there with us today to plan all the changes to the place," Kip said. "You know where it is, don't you?" he added loudly, hoping the Indian lad would hear. "It's down on the cove facing the Sandbanks."

"Yes, and your dad was telling me it has a name now. Kip's Cove. Is that it?"

"That's it." Kip was delighted at the help the storekeeper was unknowingly giving him. Now perhaps Dan Stonefish would drift into his cove in the fishing-boat with his father.

"Well, drop in on us often, Chris." Mr. Bell's eyes twinkled behind the steel-rimmed glasses. "We're always ready for business or ready for a chat."

"We'll come down for the summer when school's out," Kip promised.

"See you then!" Mr. Bell waved him out of the door.

Kip glanced over his shoulder. Dan smiled briefly but before Kip left he was again engrossed in his magazine.

4. A Noise in the Night and a New Job

Within four weeks school was out for the summer. The combined efforts of Kip and his father on the week-ends, and Mr. Mosely during the week, had made the cottage at Kip's Cove quite habitable. Despite the nights they had spent with Mr. Mosely Kip had not grown used to his abrupt manner. "It's just his way and you'll have to accept it," Mr. Brooks said after one of their overnight visits. "There are no frills about Mr. Mosely."

"I don't care about the frills," Kip grumbled, "but I sure wish he'd stop acting as if he was mad at me all the time."

Mr. Brooks smiled. "I'm afraid you're going to have to learn to take people the way you find them, Kip," he said. "Besides, you won't be seeing much more of him now that we're nearly finished down at the cove."

But Kip had other ideas and they definitely involved Mr. Mosely. He said nothing until their final night with the old sailor and the two men were discussing methods of dealing with the annual crop of dandelions.

"I do a bit of spraying for some of the bigger houses in the village," Mr. Mosely was saying. "But I don't know whether I'll get out this year or not with no help in the greenhouse."

"I could come and help!" The words were out before Kip had really reached the decision himself.

"You mean come and work for Mr. Mosely?" said Mr. Brooks, astonished.

"Sure that's what I mean! Think of all I'd learn about gardens and plants and everything!" He did not add the thought that was uppermost in his mind. Daily work in Bloomfield would increase his chances of meeting Dan a hundredfold.

"But I thought you'd want to stay at the new cottage!" Mr. Brooks sounded disappointed.

"Oh, there'd be lots of time for that," Kip said hastily. "Maybe Mr. Mosely wouldn't mind if I worked just the mornings here and spent the afternoons down at the cove." Dan was his only hope for the summer and he was determined to cross his path again.

"I haven't said you'd be suitable to me yet." Mr. Mosely probed him with cold blue eyes. "There's plenty you don't know about greenhouse work."

"But I could learn! I'd listen and do everything you told me! After all, I did a good job down at the cottage, didn't I?"

"Passable, I suppose." Mr. Mosely puffed on his pipe with slow deliberation.

Resentment flared in Kip. He would have given anything to have been able to make an angry retort. He had worked long hard hours on the new cottage and even his father had commended him. But not Mr. Mosely. Oh, no! Kip doubted if he had ever praised anybody or anything.

"Mind you, I don't suppose it's anything that you couldn't learn if you'd keep your ears and eyes open," Mr. Mosely said.

"Oh, I'd pay attention, honestly, Mr. Mosely!" Kip said. "You'd never have a better worker than me!"

"Oh?" Mr. Mosely smiled wryly.

"But how in the world would you get up here in the mornings?" Mr. Brooks asked.

"I could bike up!"

"But it's over six miles!" And yet a smile of pleasure lit Mr. Brooks' face. "Don't you think you're being a little ambitious?"

"He can ride up with Albert. I'll pay him a dollar and a half a morning. He has a lot to learn, you know." Mr. Mosely spoke as if the matter were completely settled.

"Zowie! Did you hear that, Dad? Mr. Mosely says I can come!" Kip shouted. "And I get a dollar and a half every day!"

Mr. Brooks put a hand on his shoulder. "Wait a minute now. Who is this Albert?"

"Albert Tewson, the postman," Mr. Mosely said. "He lives at the Outlet past your turn. He can pick the boy up in the morning and drop him off again on his way back after lunch. I'll speak to Albert."

Kip supposed that if Mr. Mosely spoke to Albert that would finish it. Even Albert, whatever his qualities, would not dare to oppose the old captain.

"Well, between the two of you, I can see that you've made up your minds completely about this thing," Mr. Brooks said. "But remember, we haven't spoken to your mother yet."

"Oh, Dad, you've just got to get her to say, 'yes'!" Kip said. And yet he wondered about his mother. She had never allowed him any activity that took him too far away from home. She would object to his working at all, he knew that.

Later, in his bedroom at home, he tried to stay awake to hear what was being said in the living-room. But the long hours of work and the fresh air were too much for him. He had just heard Edna's strident voice declare, "Well, if you ask me, it would be the best thing that could happen to him," when he fell asleep.

Edna was the first to greet him in the morning. "Hi!" she said. "Does the working man want porridge for breakfast this morning?"

"Do you mean Mother said I could do it?" Kip said.

"Well, it took a little persuading, but I think we have her convinced," Edna smiled. "Now all you have to do is to stick to it." She eyed him quizzically. "And that won't be easy."

"What do you mean?" Kip scoffed. "It's an easy job. Anybody could learn if they tried. After all, I'm pretty good at the carpentry now, and I bet I turn out to be a real expert at the greenhouse stuff."

"Oh, sure," Edna said. "I bet you do."

The following week-end they all drove down to Kip's Cove. Kip trod closely on his mother's heels as they climbed the hill to the house, laden with all the household paraphernalia. He wanted to see the expression on her face when she first caught sight of the new summer home. She had not been down in all their weeks of work. "I'll wait," she had said with her usual gay smile. "I love surprises."

There was no doubt of her great surprise when she broke through the clump of cedars at the crest of the hill, and little wonder for it. The wide screened verandah swept across the front of the old log school, facing the magnificent arc of West Lake beach, and the glittering dunes of the Sandbanks. The bedrooms, of log siding to harmonize with the original structure, formed two wings in the rear, giving the whole, in spite of its solidity, the appearance of a huge brown bird clinging to the summit of the hill.

Edna was following Mrs. Brooks as they mounted the slope. At the latter's long pause she gave a laughing shout. "Mrs. Brooks, dear, you'll have to move or all these pots and pans I'm carrying will end up in the lake!"

Kip's mother moved aside quickly to let her pass. "Oh, Edna, did you ever see anything like this?" She turned to Kip. "And to think you did so much of the work yourself!"

"Well, it really wasn't so hard," Kip said. "And it sure was a lot of fun. Do you like it, Edna?"

Edna staggered to the desk picnic table in the glen of ce-

dars and dropped her awkward bundle of kitchen hardware. "What's this, a fresh air school?" she asked.

"They were all inside when we first came here, Edna," Mr. Brooks explained, "and we didn't want to throw them out." He smiled. "From what Mr. Mosely said, the ghosts might object."

"Ghosts!" Edna exclaimed. "Will they expect a cup of tea and a cookie when they come? I want to be prepared."

They all laughed and followed Edna to the doorway. The

large schoolroom had been entirely made over, the walls lined
with oak and the ceiling attractively tiled. A panelled divider,
already bright with blossoms from Mr. Mosely's greenhouse,
separated the kitchen and dining area from the sitting-room.

"My bedroom's through here," Kip called. This room was
finished in pine and overlooked the little creek.

"Trust Kip to find a built-in lullaby," Edna remarked when
she heard the small singing sound of the stream. She strode
brusquely to the door. "Come on now, everybody. If we're
going to get settled today, you're all going to have to pitch in."

By late evening they had the necessities stowed away to
Edna's satisfaction. They all sat in the picnic grove watching
the darkness come down on the lake while Edna tended the
coffee pot. To Kip the cloud shapes were phantom ships sailing
up the sky, and the Sandbanks dark-rimmed isles of mystery
and legend to which he might one day adventure.

"You know what time it is, Kip?" His mother's voice broke
the silence.

"Oh, no, Mom! I don't have to go to bed yet, do I?" Kip
wailed. "It's the first night here! I'm not tired, honestly I'm
not!"

"You heard what your mother said." Mr. Brooks' voice was firm.

"Please, Mother! Just another half hour!"

"Well, perhaps, just for tonight, but it'll be early to bed tomorrow night if you're going off to a new job on Monday morning."

Edna rose. "Do you know what would do us all a world of good? A swim!"

"Hurrah! Let's go!" Kip shouted.

Later, while they were splashing and shouting together, the moon came up and turned the water to liquid silver. It made a shimmering trail to the rim of the Sandbanks on the horizon, and the cottage itself was a ghostly galleon sailing among the cedars.

"How's the swimming coming?" Mr. Brooks called to Kip.

"Okay, I guess. But I still can't do the crawl. I can't seem to get the breathing right." He wished that he could have had swimming lessons, but his mother had said that the pool was too far away from the old home. He could do the side stroke and the dog paddle, but tired easily. His mother and father were not particularly good swimmers but they enjoyed the water.

"As for me," Edna bubbled, "I'd love to teach you a thing or two, but all I can do is wallow around like an old whale!"

"Work hard at it, Kip," Mr. Brooks suggested, "and let me see some improvement when I come back next week-end."

Kip realized suddenly that it would seem strange there when his father left. In Haliburton there had been other cottages close at hand, most of them within shouting distance. Here they were isolated. The thought made him shiver, half with delight, half with a feeling that he could not define. He would be the man of the house for the entire week until his father returned.

The following night they all walked to the end of the lane to wave Mr. Brooks on his way. A feeling of loneliness seemed to possess the cove as the car disappeared round the bend.

"Gosh, it's really quiet here, isn't it?" Kip said.

"Just the way we want it," Edna said. "We can all do with a good rest, and just see that you behave yourself, skipper, and give your mother one."

"Oh, he's a good boy." Mrs. Brooks eyed him affectionately. "He won't do anything he shouldn't, even if his father isn't here."

"He'd better not." Edna's tone was bantering, but Kip knew that she meant every word. Her long-established place in the household gave her the right to mete out punishment when it was needed.

They went for a brisk hike along the shore and tried to identify the birds swooping among the reeds of a nearby swamp. Then they came in and lit the oil lamps, and the cottage became a snug fortress against the cool darkness outside.

"It'll be nice when we get the electricity in," Edna said, straining to read a magazine.

"Oh, no!" Kip said. "I love it this way. It's more like pioneering."

Nevertheless he had occasion to wish for an electric switch close at hand when the noise awakened him later in the night. He sat bolt upright in bed. He could hear the loud ticking of the old alarm clock beside Edna's couch in the living-room, and the furious beating of his own heart, but nothing more. And yet he knew there had been a noise. It came again, a furtive rustling that seemed to approach him from every corner of the room. He dove under the bedclothes and stuffed his fingers in his ears. If he lay quite still it might go away. But then, suppose it was a ghost and he missed it. He peered over the edge of the sheet. The vague familiar shapes of dresser and chair took form as his eyes grew used to the darkness. The noise came again. This time he leaped out of bed and ran across the cold floor to Edna's bed. He found it hard to waken her.

"Edna! Edna!" He shook her again and again. "I heard a noise! Maybe it's a ghost!"

"Uh?" Edna opened her eyes. "What's this?"

"Edna, it's me! I hear a funny noise and I don't know what it is!"

"A noise?" Edna sat up in bed. "What kind of noise?"

"It was like a rustling and it seemed to be all over my bedroom. Edna, do you think it's a ghost? What'll we do if it is?"

Edna reached sleepily for her robe. "Make him tea and cookies like I suggested," she said. "Don't be so noisy or you'll wake your mother."

But Mrs. Brooks was already standing in the doorway. The lamp in her hand shed a welcome light in the room. "What's the matter out here? Is someone ill?"

"Kip thinks we have ghosts, Mrs. Brooks," Edna said. "And if we have one, let's meet him and get it over with." She lit the lamp beside her bed and holding it aloft like a righteous sword, she advanced into his bedroom. "Now where is he?"

"Listen!" Kip said.

The noise came almost at once, loud and insistent, this time followed by an odd bouncing rattle. Edna looked startled and Mrs. Brooks pulled Kip close.

"What is it?" she whispered. Kip could feel her trembling. The knowledge that his mother was afraid made him feel stronger.

Edna tossed her head. "We'll soon settle that fellow," she promised. Pulling her gown tightly about her she was gone out of the side door taking the lamp with her.

"Whatever is she doing?" Mrs. Brooks asked.

"Search me," Kip said. They both watched at the window as Edna came round the corner of the house with the lamp.

"Come out of there!" they could hear her shouting. "Shoo! Shoo!"

Suddenly Kip felt like laughing. Ghost or no ghost, Edna was a comic sight standing there in her dressing-gown, angrily shaking the lamp. "A squirrel!" he shouted as a swift scuttling sounded beneath them, and a small black shape leaped from one of the air vents Mr. Mosely had made in the cottage foundation. "It was only a squirrel!"

"Thank goodness!" his mother sighed, relieved. "At least we'll know what to expect the next time."

As for Kip, he did not know whether to be glad or sorry. He half believed in Mr. Mosely's ghosts, and wondered what it would be like to meet one. Could he ask it about times past in the old school? Might it be the ghost of an Indian who had stalked the trail beside the creek? Perhaps one dark summer night there would be another noise and this time it would not be a mischievous squirrel. Perhaps . . . But Edna had re-entered the house. "That's that," she said. "One ghost well accounted for." She spoke as if accounting for ghosts was all in a day's work.

They slept in the following morning and all hands were turned towards helping Kip to be ready for the postman at the end of the lane by twenty minutes after eight. His mother wanted to come down to the road to see him off and he was vastly relieved when she was not dressed on time. After all, he was going out to do a man's job and he did not want his mother hanging about when he was going to meet a stranger.

Albert came along in his battered old car about five minutes late. He hailed Kip with a dour, "Things don't look too good to me. It'll rain before night."

Kip was mildly astonished because the clouds of the previous night had cleared and it was hot and humid.

"Haze on the horizon," Albert explained as he started the car with a roar. "Always rain with haze on the horizon. Never mind. Have to put up with it, I guess. What can't be cured must be endured."

"I guess you're right," Kip said, and felt at home with him at once.

In the days that followed Kip grew used to the abbreviated

sentences. Oddly enough their pessimism did not seem to affect Albert's fundamental cheerfulness in the least. He was a kindly man full of friendly gossip about the neighbourhood and a mine of information about the history of the Isle of Quinte.

"Saw it all in the paper," he confided to Kip. "*Picton Centennial* a few years back. Had the whole thing in the paper. Must have lost a deal of money on that paper, too," he interrupted himself. "Great bulky thing. No advertisements. Just history and local news from a hundred years back. Yes, sir. Must have lost a deal of money."

"But what about the stories in it?" Kip asked eagerly. He hated history at school, but here it was different.

"Oh, plenty of stories. Plenty. Says Champlain was one of the first to see the place. Samuel de his name was. Now that's a funny one. How'd you like a name like that?" Albert glanced at him. "Samuel de."

"He was a Frenchman. That's why he had a name like that," Kip explained. "He was one of the greatest explorers that ever came to North America."

"Oh, I know, I know." This was Albert's tale and he was not going to let Kip deprive him of it. "Said all that in the paper. This Samuel de went right up the St. Lawrence River and even got as far as Georgian Bay. Smart man."

"And what about this place?" Kip asked. "You said he saw it."

"Not only saw it," Albert said. "Put it on the map, too. Year 1612. Paper said he was the first European to navigate the Trent River and the Bay of Quinte. Did a few silly things in his time though."

Kip turned to look at Albert. "What do you mean by that?"

Albert shrugged his shoulders. "Got himself all mixed up with the Indians."

Kip grinned. "I'll bet it was hard around here in those days not to get yourself mixed up with them."

"Anyway, he led a war party of Hurons and Algonquins

against the Iroquois in the Mohawk Valley. Iroquois turned right round and chased them back. Big battles here in Prince Edward County between Huron and Iroquois. Wiped out the Huron missions. Funny thing. Indians fighting right here where we're driving, eh?"

Yes, Kip thought, it was a funny thing, but not hard to imagine the rolling farm land green with forests and sewn with Indian trails.

"Take that tree down the road there. Wishing-tree. Paper says it's seven hundred years old!"

"You mean that one down by the corner?" Kip leaned forward as they approached. It had once been an enormous tree skirted by the road, but now all that remained were two jagged remnants of trunk pointing gnarled fingers to the sky. Yet the huge girth of the tree could be seen plainly. A giant maple, it had succumbed to lightning years before.

"That's the one." Albert drew to a stop beside it. "Wishing-tree."

Kip was puzzled. "How do you mean?"

Albert felt in his pocket for a bag of gumdrops. He offered one to Kip. "Just means what it says. For wishing, that tree. Indians used to dance around it. Held their arrows against it to make them good shooters. Even took a piece of bark in their hands, made a wish and stuck the bark back in the hole. Came true, too."

"Oh, that's just baby stuff," Kip laughed. "It's like fairy tales. You don't believe that when you get older."

Albert pursed his lips. "Wouldn't be too sure. Tried it myself once. It worked."

Kip eyed him, unbelieving. "You're fooling."

"Sure as I'm sitting here. Wished I'd get the postman's job. Here I am!"

"Gee!" Kip stared at the tree. "I don't suppose it would work for me," he said.

"Don't see why not," Albert said. "No harm in trying."

No harm if no one but Albert saw him doing it. He could imagine the scorn of Mike or Brian back at the old place if they could see him. He would never hear the last of it. But still, Albert was a grown man and he had tried it. "I think I will," Kip said. "Will you wait?"

"You bet. Take your time."

Kip glanced hurriedly about to make sure no one was watching. He stepped out of the car and ran to the tree. He tore a piece of bark from the tree and held it tightly, trying to think of the right words. But only two came. Dan Stonefish. Dan Stonefish. Almost a week had passed at Mr. Mosely's greenhouse and as often as he had found an excuse to go to the store, he had never seen Dan again. He found a narrow fissure in the wood and pushed the fragment of bark into it. Then he ran back to the car.

"Tell me when you get it," Albert said. "You will."

Kip still felt rather foolish. "Sure," he said.

He wondered the next day if it might not have been wiser to have made a wish for some drastic change in Mr. Mosely's personality. The first few days had not been too hard. The old man had explained things to him in the usual sparse manner, and Kip had tried to follow instructions to the letter. But it seemed there was always something he was not doing right. This time it was the zinnia shoots. He was transplanting them from the greenhouse bed to the small buyer's baskets when he heard his employer's crisp voice behind him.

"You've planted all those too deep. They'll all have to come out again."

"All of them?" Kip surveyed the ten baskets lined up before him.

"All of them. You'll kill them with soil. Take more care the next time and do it properly."

"But it looked just the way you showed me!" Kip said.

"Well, it isn't." Mr. Mosely turned away. "I have a buyer coming for fifteen boxes this afternoon, so don't waste time."

"I'll waste as much as I like," Kip thought angrily. But he bit his lip and said nothing. The heat pouring into the greenhouse from the July sun was almost unbearable, and there he was with ten boxes to empty and fill again. If it were not for Dan Stonefish, he would tell Mr. Mosely exactly what he thought of him and leave. He had known working with the greenhouse keeper would not be easy, but surely a word or two of praise would not hurt him.

When he walked on his way to meet Albert after lunch, kicking a stone before him under the shadows of the trees on the main street, he wished that he had never become involved with Mr. Mosely. What was the use when Dan Stonefish never appeared to cross his path? He leaned against a tree, picking at the bark. Suddenly he saw a figure flying down the road on a bicycle. The black hair and long lean body were instantly familiar. It was Dan Stonefish! "I'll stop him and tell him I got a job at Mr. Mosely's!" Kip thought joyfully. "Then maybe he'll come and see me." But suddenly another thought leaped into his mind. The job! He had taken the Indian boy's job at the greenhouse! Perhaps Dan had wanted to work to help his family, and Kip had taken his place. It was strange that he had not considered this before, but he had been much too intent on his own ends to think of Dan and his needs. Dan would have heard by now that Kip had the job because everybody knew everything up at the store. Would he be annoyed or disappointed?

The bicycle drew nearer, little whorls of dust following in its wake. Kip hesitated in the shadows of the maple. Then suddenly it was too late. Dan was gone up the main street, a whirl of pedals and brown jeans. Albert arrived a few moments later and Kip, in his dejection, answered him only in monosyllables all the way home. Even Edna could not persuade him to go in for a swim. He went, instead, to his room and flung himself on the bed. He wished that they had never come to Kip's Cove. Nothing had really turned out right for him from the start. All he had got out of it was a lot of hard work. Of course, there was the swimming every afternoon with Edna and his mother and the long hikes up the beach. But who wanted to swim and hike with two women? It was a boy he needed, someone with whom he could share the good times that came only with summer. It was true that even with a week not yet past his mother was looking happier and more rested, and Edna was as gay as a lark, varying their meals with roasts at the beach and sandwiches at the picnic table. But neither of them gave a thought to him and his needs. He remembered with a pang of self pity, all the fun that John and Peter were having without him at this very minute up in Haliburton. If he could just have had a dog things would not be so bad. He wondered where Dan's dog was. Tad. That was his name. A good name for a dog. Tad.

If his employer noticed any difference in him in the next day or two he did not remark upon it. Friday morning arrived with the same hot glaring sky that had made the air in the greenhouse simmer all week long. Mr. Mosely's greeting was brief as usual.

"Good morning," he said. "The tomato bed needs weeding and the rose bed has to be sprayed. Use the spray you mixed up on Monday, the one beside the flower pots."

Kip did not know how he came to use the wrong solution. He was very hot and tired after the long week, and he was not thinking about his job, he had to admit that to himself later. At any rate, when Mr. Mosely came upon him an hour later, he froze in his tracks at the old man's tone of voice.

"I see this yellow tin's empty," he said. "Is this what you used in the spray?"

"Yes," Kip said, "it's the one I mixed on Monday, isn't it?"

"No," said Mr. Mosely, "that happens to be in the green tin. Didn't you hear what I said? The one beside the flower pots."

"Yes, but I thought . . ."

"You obviously didn't think at all, that's the trouble. Now

get a water solution and wash that stuff off before it kills all my roses."

Kip's cheeks flamed. He faced the older man, his eyes blazing. "Wash it off yourself," he shouted. "I'm sick of the whole thing! If I can't do anything right, then do it all alone!"

He flung the spray can to the ground. It gave a loud clatter as he plunged out of the greenhouse and ran down the path. He ran and ran, wanting only to get as far away from the greenhouse as possible. Presently, bathed in perspiration, he came to the road that branched off the main street. It was the long winding way to West Lake and Kip's Cove. He slackened his pace. The greenhouse was now far behind him and he would never have to see Mr. Mosely again. Resentment seethed in him. He had wanted to answer Mr. Mosely back all those long hours of work at the cottage and the greenhouse. He had done it and he was not sorry. That would teach him to go around ordering other people about. He didn't have to work anyway, and take all Mr. Mosely's orders. He wasn't like Dan who probably needed the money for his family. His own father had lots of money and he could have anything he wanted. Well, almost anything. He had noticed lately that his mother did not so easily give way to him. All he knew now was that he hated Mr. Mosely and he never wanted to see him and his old greenhouse again.

He was so concerned with himself that he did not see the clouds, gray and towering, massing in the sky like a great army preparing to do battle. When the thunder crashed over him with the sound of a hundred barrels rolling down a mountain, he looked up with a start. A jagged knife of lightning split the sky. The rain came in a torrent, soaking him to the skin almost at once. It was such an enormous relief to be cool again that he wanted to shout, but he knew he should seek some shelter from the storm. There was a barn close by the fence that bordered the wheat field. He wondered if the farmer would mind if he stayed there until the storm was over. He headed for the fence, almost blinded by the force of the water, when suddenly, in the strange semi-twilight of the morning, he saw a car approaching. Its headlights were on and it was doing little more than moving through the downpour.

Kip recognized his father's car at once. He was shocked at its sudden appearance. As yet he had not thought at all of how to justify his behaviour. He even wondered briefly if he should hide and take his time on the six miles home so that he could rehearse his opening speech. But the car had stopped. His father had seen him.

Mr. Brooks' opening remarks were jocular enough. "Well," he began when the door had slammed shut, "it looks like a good hot bath for you when you get home. I needed a periscope to find you out there."

Kip managed a half smile. He said nothing because he did not know what to say. It was even worse when they reached the cottage. His mother greeted him with astonishment but Edna said a mere "Hi!" and began to fill the tub with steaming water from the stove. Despite the previous heat the water was comforting, for a cold wind, the aftermath of the storm, was whipping across the lake. He wished that someone would question him or scold him, but no one ventured a remark about his unexpected appearance at home at this hour of the morning. He sat in his bedroom, warm and dry in clean jeans and a long-sleeved jersey, wondering how to begin.

He opened the bedroom door. Mr. Brooks, who had been reading a magazine in a nearby corner, sprang to his feet as a sudden ray of sunlight glowed in the room. "The sun's coming out! The storm must be over!" He opened the front door and walked to the verandah.

The cottage was filled at once with the close thunder of the waves. As far as they could see across West Lake and south to the Sandbanks, they came riding into shore like an army of white-plumed knights. The wind blew steadily from the west, shaking a million raindrops from the branches in the woods.

"I'm off for a walk," Mr. Brooks said. "I'll be back when all the cobwebs are blown away." He slipped on his sports jacket and was gone out of the door.

Kip picked up a book and pretended to read. Inwardly he was fuming. Why did his father not ask him what had happened? Why did they all act as if it were the most natural thing in the world for him to be home at this hour in the morning? Edna and his mother had gone to the verandah. Should he join them there and start up a conversation so that he could explain how mean Mr. Mosely had been to him? Suddenly he flung the book down and went to the bedroom to fetch his jacket. He would go and find his father and make a beginning there. He could afford to be a little more dramatic without Edna around. He slipped quietly out of the back door and hastened to the beach, the sodden grass making a squelching sound beneath his running shoes. His father was nowhere in sight. Kip ran along, the wind whipping his face, to the tip of the point that formed the cove on the northern side. He looked beyond it. There was no trace of his father even here. He turned slowly and walked towards the spot where the little creek tumbled into the lake. Willet's Creek. He remembered the name with displeasure. He leaped across the narrow bed and began to walk slowly into the woods. Maybe he would not even go in for lunch. He would make them wonder where he was, and then they would all come out looking for him. They would be sorry then that they had been so mean to him. But suddenly he knew where his father was even before he broke through the trees. He could smell the fragrance of his tobacco smoke drifting through the leaves.

His father was standing, hands deep in his pockets, pipe in his mouth, looking down at the little pond in the clearing. In this place there was no breath of the boisterous wind out on the beach, and the sound of waves was muted by the surrounding bush.

"Hello, Kip," Mr. Brooks said. "All dry now?"

"Yes, I'm dry," Kip said. He kicked at a fallen log. "I'm not going back to Mr. Mosely's," he added quickly.

"Oh?"

Kip turned with a torrent of words. "I'll bet he's just about the meanest person anybody ever worked for! He's always bawling me out for things, and never says I do anything good! I hate him and I hope I never have to see him again!" He was about to add that he hated Kip's Cove, too, but something told him that he had said enough.

"I took an extra day with the week-end and when I got down here this morning, I understood from your mother that you were getting along very well at the greenhouse," Mr. Brooks observed. "I was just on my way up to see you and take you and Mr. Mosely out to lunch down at the motel."

"I wouldn't go out to lunch with him. I wouldn't do anything with him or for him again!"

Mr. Brooks sat down on the log. "Tell me something. These things he bawled you out for, as you put it, were they your fault?"

Kip bit his lip and was silent.

"Well, were they?"

"I did make a few mistakes. But they weren't that important."

Mr. Brooks did not take his gaze from Kip's face. "And what happened this morning?"

"Oh, some old thing." Kip shrugged his shoulders. "I can hardly remember what it was."

"I think you can remember very well," Mr. Brooks said. "I would like to know."

Kip felt the tears very close to the surface. He was chagrined that his father had brought him to the point of confession. And yet there was no other way out. "I sprayed the roses with the wrong stuff," he blurted out, "but there were so many old tins around there, how's anybody to know what to use?"

"But didn't Mr. Mosely tell you what to use?"

"Sure, I guess he did."

Mr. Brooks rose. "You mean you know he did. Spraying roses with the wrong solution can be a pretty fatal error. Surely you couldn't blame Mr. Mosely for being annoyed. Did you say you were sorry?"

Kip did not answer.

"You mean you didn't even apologize?" Mr. Brooks looked shocked. "Kip, don't you realize that you've taken on a man's job and you've got to be treated like one? You're not a baby any more."

"You bet I'm not a baby. I'm nearly twelve years old!"

"Then you'll have to start acting like it," Mr. Brooks said.

Kip had not thought of it this way before. He considered his father's statement. "But why does he always sound so mad at me, even when I haven't done anything? He never says more than he has to."

"I've told you, Kip, you have to take people the way you find them. As the captain of a lake freighter, I imagine Mr. Mosely had no time to waste words. His whole life is geared to his speech. Did you notice how practical his house is and everything in it?"

Yes, Kip had noticed that. The house had contained no more than the bare necessities, and these had been spotless.

"Don't you think that Mr. Mosely did you quite a favour taking you on when you'd never worked before?" Mr. Brooks went on. "After all, perhaps if he'd waited another week the Indian lad would have been back, or someone else with experience."

Kip's cheeks grew hot as he remembered the spray can lying on the greenhouse floor. "I don't know what to do now," he mumbled.

"I think we both know what you should do," Mr. Brooks said.

"You mean go back? But I couldn't, Dad! What would I say?"

"To say you're sorry might be a good beginning," Mr. Brooks said.

"But he'll be terribly mad," Kip objected. "What will he do?"

"You'll have to go and find that out for yourself." His father sounded completely unsympathetic, but then, when he talked to Mr. Mosely it was man to man, not man to boy.

"Golly, I don't know what to do," Kip said mournfully. "I didn't think about having to go back. I guess I was kind of rude." He pulled a piece of moss apart in his fingers. "Well, okay, I'll go up with Albert tomorrow morning."

"Kip, during the war when we were training to be pilots, if one of us was ever in a crash and escaped unhurt, do you know what our instructors did?"

"No, what?"

"They sent us up in another plane the moment we reported back to the hangar."

Kip stared at his father. He rose slowly. "Will you take me up now before lunch?"

"Let's go!" Mr. Brooks set off down the path to the beach and Kip followed.

His mother and Edna asked no questions and for that he was grateful. He did not think he could go through all that again. All the way up in the car he was wondering what angry frame of mind he would find Mr. Mosely in when he arrived.

"Here we are," his father called out. "Do you need me?"

Kip hesitated. "No. No, thanks, Dad, I'll manage," he said.

"Tell Mr. Mosely I'll come and pick you both up in an hour," Mr. Brooks suggested. "I'll go and have a chat with Mr. Bell up at the store."

Kip stood watching the car drive up the street. Then he walked resolutely up the path to the greenhouse behind the frame cottage. Mr. Mosely was nowhere in sight. He must be still in the greenhouse, Kip thought. He stood in the doorway and caught sight of Mr. Mosely at the far end. His head was bent over something and he had a screwdriver in his hand. As Kip advanced slowly he saw that the something was the spray can. He would have given anything to have been able to turn and run. He did not know how he would approach the old man. Quickly he tried a few phrases to himself. *Hello, Mr. Mosely, I'm back. . . . I'm sorry, Mr. Mosely, I won't do it again. . . . If I broke the spray can I'll pay for it, Mr. Mosely.*

When the old man lifted his head and spoke suddenly, Kip was startled. "I see this handle's come loose," he said. "It's all right now. You can start to work on the tomato plants any time."

That was all there was to it. Kip stared after him with a great surge of relief and gratitude as he ambled slowly down the greenhouse to the tins of spraying solution. "Spray for the tomatoes is in the white tin," he called over his shoulder. "I have to see what damage the storm did to the arbour. I'll be back in a minute."

Kip set to work as if his life depended upon it. A sudden rush of liking for the old man welled up in him. There he was with every opportunity in the world to bawl him out and he had not said a word.

His father, as always, had been right.

5. To Find the Frenchman's Gold

Lunch at the motel was, for Kip, something of a celebration. At the beginning he felt that he could not raise his eyes to meet those of his employer, but since the latter acted as if nothing had happened, Kip soon relaxed. Mr. Brooks made them both feel at ease by plying the greenhouse keeper with questions about the surrounding district.

"This is going to be a favourite haunt of ours we hope for a good many years," Mr. Brooks said. "I'd like to get to know it better."

"Maybe you've heard some of our Indian legends," Mr. Mosely said. "Has Albert been talking to you?"

"Albert tells me a lot," Kip said, "but nothing about legends."

"Then you haven't heard the one about the Lake on the Mountain. Have you been up there yet?"

"No," Mr. Brooks put in, "but we must take a drive there. I hear the view is pretty fine out over the bay."

"Yes, and it's a bit of an oddity, that lake. It's away up there above water level and nobody has been able to figure out where the water comes from up so high."

"Maybe it was a mystery to the Indians, too," Kip said, "and that's why they made stories about it."

"It's possible," Mr. Mosely agreed. "That lake was a favourite camping ground for some of the Mohawk tribe. When the hunting season rolled round every year they camped by the lake to fish and hunt and make war on anybody round about. The daughter of the chief was quite a beauty from all accounts. Tayouroughay was her name. She loved a chief of her own tribe, one of the lesser ones you might say, whose name was Gowanda. Pretty fancy names they had," he added with one of his rare smiles.

"Hard to say, too!" Kip laughed. He was astonished at Mr. Mosely. He had never heard him say so much at one time before.

Mr. Mosely went on. "Everyone thought Gowanda had been killed. He had never returned from a hunting party in the far land to the east. It seems there was another brave who wanted to marry the Indian princess. His name was Annosothka. That means Black Snake in Mohawk. This fellow was the chief of a strong tribe to the north. The princess' father thought it might be a good idea to have her marry him so that the tribe in the north would be his ally in war." Mr. Mosely shrugged his shoulders. "In those days daughters did what their fathers told them. And it was decided that Tayouroughay should marry Annosothka."

"That would mean a big feast," Kip said, sipping his chocolate milk shake. "Dancing and beating tom-toms and stuff like that."

Mr. Mosely nodded. "That's just the way it was, and the girl's father called in Black Snake and his tribe to help them to celebrate. Well, they were all shouting and singing and dancing by the lake-shore with a huge fire blazing among them, and what do you suppose was happening down in the bay below?"

"I couldn't imagine," Mr. Brooks said. "Tell us."

"Far down the bay there was a lone canoe coming up the water and in that canoe sat Gowanda. His band of hunters had all been captured and killed but he had managed to escape after torture and starvation."

"Perhaps when he saw the fire on the mountain he thought it was to light him home," Kip said.

"Perhaps. But he climbed up the mountain and hid in the bushes to watch the marriage feast. As he watched, a big snake, drawn by the fire, slithered out in front of the princess. He sprang from the bushes and killed it, then made off to a nearby island."

"And what did the princess do?" Kip asked.

"She took her own canoe and followed him. Black Snake called her to come back but she never came. Black Snake called his tribe to him and told them that this was the will of the Great Manitou. He warned them to keep the peace with Tayouroughay's tribe as long as the leaves should grow on the trees around the mountain lake. Then he leaped into the lake and was never seen again."

"Gee, poor Black Snake," Kip said.

"You know," Mr. Mosely added, "the Indians say that if you listen hard up there on the mountain at twilight, you can hear the leaves of the trees whisper the girl's name. Even the Indians had their romantic nonsense by the sound of it."

Kip didn't know about it being nonsense. He rather liked the idea. The Lake on the Mountain had become more than ever a spot to visit. He clearly remembered his father's mention of it in connection with some mysterious cave in the mountain side. He was jubilant at Mr. Mosely's next words.

"I have to go up there next week some time to take some plants for the restaurant. If the boy likes he can come with me."

"Oh, I'd like that all right, Mr. Mosely!" Kip exclaimed. "And there's something else I want to know. Once, down at the cove, you said there was a treasure at the Outlet. What did you mean by that?"

"Don't you think Mr. Mosely's done quite enough tale-telling for one day, Kip?" Mr. Brooks smiled. "You might give him a little rest."

"If the boy's to be part of the place, he might as well know it all," Mr. Mosely said. "The story goes that there's a barrel of gold buried down at the Outlet. It was laid there in the Seven Years War between France and England."

"A barrel of gold!" Kip's eyes widened. "Boy! How did anybody come to bury a barrel of gold? It sounds like pirates!"

"It was the French. They ruled the island here from Fort Frontenac in those days. That's Kingston now. The English sailed up the bay to attack the fort and on the way gave chase to a French gunboat. They say the French ship was chased for thirty miles along the south shore of the county, and then the French captain got desperate, beached his ship round Salmon Point, set fire to it, and buried his gold."

"Why hasn't anybody dug for it?" Kip asked.

"Knowing human nature, I imagine somebody has!" Mr. Brooks put in.

"They have, right enough, all over the Outlet, but there's miles of beach down there and nobody has ever found the right place," Mr. Mosely said.

"But you're a captain yourself," Kip burst out. "You must have an idea where it's buried."

"I've often thought of trying one particular spot," the old sailor agreed. "There's a little sand dune off the others at the end of the beach, just where East Lake comes down in a creek to Lake Ontario. It's close to where the ship must have rounded the point at any rate."

"We'll all go and dig for it tomorrow," Mr. Brooks laughed.

"I wouldn't scoff at such tales," said Mr. Mosely. "There

have been plenty of strange things found around here, and if ever there was a cradle of Canadian history, this is it."

"Well, I sure believe in buried treasure and things like that," Kip said. "I'd even like to dig for it myself." He did not add that a plan was already forming in his mind, one that could bring them all fame and fortune. Perhaps, if things worked out successfully, Dan Stonefish might hear of his exploits!

He tried out his plan on his family as soon as they were back at the cove. They were all sitting in the cedar glen, sheltered from the cool northwest wind that sent clouds scudding across the sky.

"Fancy going in for a swim today," Edna said. She was patching a pair of Kip's jeans. "I'd be taking the hot-water bottle in with me!"

"It would certainly wash away all your troubles out there," Mrs. Brooks said.

"I think ours have been washed away already." Edna glanced quickly down at Kip who was curled up on the grass. She gave him a swift wink.

She's guessed everything about this morning, Kip thought. He knew she would. He remembered suddenly what she had said. *Now all you have to do is to stick to it, and that won't be easy.* Well, it hadn't been easy, but he had not let her down. He was back on the job again. Now all he had to do was to find the right moment to tell Mr. Mosely he was sorry for the things he had said. He knew he would have to do it. He would feel uncomfortable until the whole affair was properly closed. In the meantime he could go ahead with his Outlet scheme.

He tried to sound casual. "You know what I'd like to do?" he said.

Mr. Brooks smiled at him. "I believe the usual answer to that is, 'No, what?' " he said.

"I'd like to take my bike up to town on Albert's car and ride it back after work," Kip said.

Mrs. Brooks dropped her magazine in her lap. "All that way! Kip, it must be six miles or more!"

"But it's pavement and pretty straight going!" Kip told her.

"Straight going!" Mrs. Brooks exclaimed. "Why, the road is one curve after another!"

"I mean there are no hills," Kip said, "and there's hardly any traffic at all in the week-days."

He found a sudden ally in his father. "The exercise certainly won't hurt him, Bet. I don't think he gets enough of it standing about in the greenhouse all morning."

"He's getting ambitious all of a sudden," Edna said. "Don't let's stand in his way." And yet she gave him a curious glance as if she knew there was more to it than that.

"Then I can do it? Can I take it up on Monday morning?" Kip begged.

"Oh, Allan, do you really think he should?" Mrs. Brooks' thin face was creased with anxiety. "It's so far all alone."

"He's got to learn to stand on his own feet some time," Mr. Brooks said. "He's nearly twelve. I think it wouldn't do him any harm to bike every day."

"Every day!" This was more than Kip had bargained for. "Gee, I didn't mean every day. I just thought I'd try it on Monday, that's all."

"Well, if you really think it's all right." She forced a smile. "I'll try to stop myself from hiking up the road to look for him."

"Yippee!" Kip bounded to his feet. "I'll be okay, Mom, I promise! But don't expect me home too soon. It'll take me a while."

Edna looked at him shrewdly but she said nothing.

Monday morning was clear and warm. "A perfect day for treasure-seeking!" Kip thought as he dressed by the open window. He was so keyed up with the prospect of it that he could scarcely choke down any breakfast.

Edna frowned at the pancakes left on his plate. "Well," she said, "it's just as well you're not biking up to work, or I'd need to run alongside with a few sugar lumps to keep you going!"

She put his lunch pail on the table. "Make sure you eat all that lunch or you'll never make it back."

"Okay, I will." Kip gulped his milk, bade them both a hasty good-bye and hurried to the tool shed to pick up his bicycle. He was delighted when he heard Edna's words as he closed the door behind him. "Come on, Mrs. Brooks, let's take our coffee out to the verandah and enjoy the morning air." That meant they wouldn't see him tying the spade to the side of his bike. He had to have a spade. You certainly couldn't dig for a barrel of gold with your bare fingers. He carried a length of rope left over from Edna's clothes-line to tie the bicycle to the car, and made off quickly down the slope to the lane.

Albert's car was already waiting for him at the end of it. The postman greeted him with raised eyebrows. "What have we got here?" he asked. " 'Fraid the old flivver will give out?"

Kip laughed. "I'm going to have the fun of biking back home today, Albert," he said. "You won't have to wait for me after lunch."

"Must be some digging going on in that greenhouse today." Albert stared at the spade. "Need extra supplies, eh?"

"Oh, it'll come in handy," Kip grinned. "I'm going to do some digging of my own today."

The excitement of the day's adventure had buoyed him up so much that he even found the courage to approach Mr. Mosely immediately he arrived. "Mr. Mosely," he began, "I want to say thank you for taking me back." He stumbled a little over the words. "And I'm really sorry for what I did the other day, especially about the spray can."

Mr. Mosely's eyes seemed to be looking right through him. "You like it here?"

"Oh, yes! Yes, I do! It's the first real job I've had. I wouldn't give it up for anything!" And he meant it. There was a new feeling, as his father had said, of being a man doing a man's job.

"You can pick some of that lettuce this morning and take

it up to the store," Mr. Mosely said, and that was the end of the matter.

When lunch was finished and the last few chores done among the plants, Kip set off gaily on his bicycle. The sun was hot and he stopped half a mile down the road to West Lake at a little creek to splash water on his face. He came up to get on his bicycle again when Albert's car drew to a stop beside him.

"Want to change your mind?" Albert drawled. "Kind of a warm day."

Kip calculated quickly. If Albert gave him a ride to his house he would be practically at the Outlet. That meant he could do his digging, find the treasure, and not be so late home. "I'll come," he decided, "but I'd like you to take me with you down to the Outlet today, please, Albert."

"Sure. Glad of the company," Albert said. He glanced at the spade. "Goin' to find the Frenchman's gold?"

It was no use. Albert had guessed. "I'm going to try. Mr. Mosely says it's really down there and I'd believe him any time."

"Looked for it myself a dozen times," Albert said as they drove off. "No luck yet. Figure somebody'll find it some day. You may be the one."

"Sure, I may be." Kip glowed. Albert had raised his hopes to a peak.

"Come and give me a shout when you find it," Albert said quite seriously. "I'll fetch the wheelbarrow."

A bar of land projected into Lake Ontario, cradling East Lake against it. It was this bar of land that was known as the Outlet, and Albert's home was just at its rim. When Kip had said good-bye to Albert and was skimming down the road, he marvelled at the amount of sand around him. The large rolling dunes formed a great wall topped with tall poplars, now like a parade of graceful grey ladies as the wind from the larger lake revealed the silvery underside of their leaves. Kip rode to the end of the arm and crossed the little wooden bridge over the narrow channel of water that flowed from East Lake to Little Sandy Bay. The water in the stream was brown and placid, the cedars and green banks mirrored within it. He turned right off the bridge and sought the point, as Albert had directed him. He saw the little island at the end of the point immediately. He flung himself off his bicycle and raced to the water's edge. He was glad when he saw its depth that he had put his bathing trunks on under his jeans. Before he stepped into the water with the spade he gazed around him. There was no one near. Even the magnificent sweep of sand beach that formed the Outlet Provincial Park was deserted. He felt suddenly very alone and thought how fine it would have been if the dog he longed for could have been beside him to share his adventure.

He took every step with caution. He was within a few feet of the island when, startled, he turned his head as he heard sudden voices around the bend in the point. "Fishermen!" There was only time for the thought to flash through his mind when he plummeted down. He had stepped into a deep hole in the sand. His mouth and throat and lungs seemed to be filled with water. He beat the water frantically with his arms while he tried to get a breath. His whole being was suffocated but when he came to the surface he managed one feeble shout. "Help!" It seemed an age as the water closed over his face again, but it was only a moment until he felt strong arms on his own, and he was half lifted, half dragged over the side of the boat. Coughing and spluttering he tried to speak at once. "I can swim!" he gasped. "It's just that I couldn't get my breath."

"There's lots of time to get it now, so lie still for a minute."

He knew the voice at once. The dark face was bending over him when he opened his eyes. It was Dan Stonefish.

Kip struggled to sit up. "I'm sorry," he said. "Sorry about the . . ." He had meant to say sorry about the job he had taken from the boy.

W. Wheeler

But Dan's father spoke behind him. "It could have happened to anybody. Don't talk for a minute. Drink this and you'll feel better."

Kip sat up slowly and took the cup of tea, hot and sweet from the thermos. The warmth of it pouring down his throat made him feel better at once. "That sure was a stupid thing to do," he said. And he remembered with chagrin the day he had fallen down the steps in front of Dan. What would the Indian boy think of him, making such a great fool of himself every time they met?

Dan smiled in a friendly fashion. "It isn't a good idea to swim alone in water you don't know. You should always bring someone with you."

"I wasn't really swimming," Kip said. "I came to dig for the treasure. And now I've lost my shovel, and my folks aren't going to be very happy about that."

Dan held the spade aloft, grinning. "I rescued it for you. But honestly, I don't think you're going to get much by digging out there. We've all tried and nobody's found a sign of it yet."

"Maybe the two of you should get together. You might have

better luck at it," Mr. Stonefish said. "But for now I think we'd
better head for shore. Dan got a little damp, too."

Kip stared at Dan's soaking blue jeans and knew that the
Indian boy had leaped in to rescue him. He did not know how
to say thank you to a boy who had saved his life. "If you let
me off on the beach," he said hurriedly, "I'll dress and bike on
home. I'll be all right. I feel fine now."

Mr. Stonefish shook his head decidedly. "We couldn't let
you do that. We'll wait until you're in your clothes, and then
we'll row round the point to Soup Harbour. That's where we
parked the car. We'll tie the boat up to the dock and drive
you home."

Despite Kip's protests that was what happened. Dan and
his father tried to draw him into conversation, but Kip's mind
was centred on what he could say to his mother and Edna if
they should see him drive up the lane in a strange car.

"Maybe we could get together sometime and teach you how
to handle yourself in the water in case of emergencies," Dan
said. "There's not much to it."

"Oh, that would be super!" Kip said. But there, too soon,
was his bend in the road. "Will you let me off at the highway,
please? The lane isn't very long and I'll make it fine."

"If that's what you want." Mr. Stonefish glanced towards
his son.

Kip realized the impression that his words had made. They
thought he did not want them to come to his home! "It's just
that . . . well . . ." he began to stammer an explanation, fearful of losing Dan at the very moment of finding him. "You see,
nobody knows I took the shovel and went down there today.
I don't want Edna and Mom to see me." An enormous envy
of Dan swept over him. He imagined this boy did not have to
make explanations for every move he took. He must be all of
fourteen years old.

"Oh, that's all right," Mr. Stonefish smiled. "We like to know
where Dan is going, too. Time enough to make up your own

mind when you're twenty-one and on your own." He opened the car door and got out to unfasten the bicycle. "The next time maybe it would be a good idea to tell them."

"Yes sir," Kip said. "I sure will."

"See you again!" Dan shouted, and the car was gone up the highway.

"Yes, but he never said when," Kip thought. Then he put his mind to getting the spade into the tool shed without Edna or his mother seeing him. He knew it would be a risky venture because they both might be in the house.

There was no one in sight at the window as he pushed the bicycle through the trees at the top of the hill and hastily opened the tool shed door. The house seemed to have a thousand eyes as he threw the spade inside and walked with exaggerated nonchalance towards the back door.

Edna was at the stove making a pudding for supper as he came in. "And how did the ride home go?" she said, smiling.

"Wonderful!" Kip felt a slow red mount his cheeks in spite of himself and he turned away. "Where's Mom?"

"Out on the verandah doing her best not to run down the lane to look for you." Edna gave him another quick glance. "You'd better go out and tell her you're safe and sound."

But his mother had heard his voice. She came in quickly. "Thank goodness you're home, dear. Are you worn out?"

"Oh, no. Not a bit," Kip said. "I feel fine. Maybe I won't take the bike again though, if it worries you." He felt more uneasiness, knowing that it was because he did not intend to search for more treasure, and not because of his mother at all.

"Have a glass of milk and a cookie, dear," Mrs. Brooks suggested. "Then maybe in an hour we'll all go in for a dip."

Kip shivered. "Not for a dip, not today," he thought. "I . . . I don't feel much like swimming today," he blurted out. "I think maybe I'll sit out in the grove and read."

He felt Edna's eyes upon him. "Well," he added lamely, "it was a long bike ride, remember?"

"Uh huh." Edna put his glass of milk before him and said nothing more.

"Of course it was, Kip," Mrs. Brooks said. "How is the work going at the greenhouse?"

"Fine. Mr. Mosely said there'll be more work than ever for the next week or two." Now why did he tell that deliberate lie? Mr. Mosely had said no such thing. But if he wanted to seek Dan out again there would have to be a reason for not getting home.

"You really like it down here now, don't you?" His mother sounded happy.

"You bet I do." That at least he could say truthfully. He never tired of sitting on the hill-top among the cedars, his knees hunched up to his chin, watching the clouds sail up the sky like the *bateaux* of the settlers of old. Sometimes in the half light of dusk he would picture the children of that long ago time trooping along the forest trail to the school and listening, as they wrote their sums laboriously in their copybooks, for the cry of an Indian. And all the time in his imaginings, a dog lay beside him, and if he put out his hand he would feel the soft warm shaggy coat and the tongue rough on his skin. Edna and his mother did not know it but always when they romped and leaped in the water, the dog was there, too, and when Kip raced along the shore in the sunlight, the sand flying behind him, the dog raced beside him. And now, of course, there was Dan. At last they had spoken together and the possibility of Dan's friendship seemed very real and close at hand.

"I'm so glad you're happy." Mrs. Brooks' pleasure was so genuine that the enormity of all his little lies and deceptions overcame him.

"I feel kind of tired," he mumbled. "I think I'll stretch out on the bed for a while." He closed the door quickly and flung himself across the quilt. Suddenly, as he remembered what the outcome of the day's adventure might have been, he was very cold and hugged the quilt close. He plugged his ears with his fingers and screwed his eyes tight shut, trying to escape from the sound of his own voice telling lies. There was a soft rap on the door and it opened quietly. He sat up throwing the quilt aside. "Hi, Edna!" He forced a grin.

"How do you do?" Edna sat on the bed. "Well, out with it, skipper. Where have you been and what happened?"

"How do you know I've been anywhere and that anything happened?" Kip got up and pretended to be very interested in the squirrels outside the window.

"You know better than to ask me that," Edna said.

"Well, I was only doing it so I could surprise you. How was I to know something would go wrong?"

"Doing what?"

"I went down to the Outlet to dig for the treasure. That's why I wanted to take my bike today," Kip confessed. "But I'm okay now. Don't worry about me."

"What do you mean, you're okay now? Young man, will you please explain to me what's been going on?" Edna stood before him, hands on hips, and he knew he would have to tell the whole story. When he had finished, she sat down again suddenly.

"Do you mean to say you nearly drowned?" Edna exclaimed.

"Well, I guess I did. But I can swim, Edna! I just couldn't get my breath because my mouth was full of water!"

Edna covered her face briefly with her hands. Then she spoke quietly. "Thank God for that Indian lad and his father. Whatever your father will be able to do to thank them, I don't know."

"Edna, you're not going to tell Mom and Dad about it!" Kip stood up, horrified.

"What else is there to do? They have to know!"

"But they don't!" Kip wailed. "Mother will never let me leave the cottage alone again if she knows. I bet she'll even make me quit the job at the greenhouse! You just wait and see!"

"There's that to it, I suppose." Edna looked worried. "You

put me in a very awkward position, Kip. I don't know what to do."

"Edna, if you don't tell, I promise I'll never do anything like that again, running off and not telling you, I mean."

"Yes, but will you keep your promise, that's what I want to know." Edna stood and faced him.

"Yes, I will! Honestly I will, Edna! Please don't tell!" Kip pleaded. "I won't even run off and see Dan without telling them."

"You won't what?" Edna frowned, puzzled.

"I was really planning to stay longer up in town so I could see if I could meet up with Dan again. That's why I said there was going to be more work at the greenhouse. But that was all a lie!" Kip felt a vast relief at his confession. "I won't do anything I'm not supposed to, and I won't go in the water again unless somebody's around."

Edna smiled. "Well, it sounds as if you really mean to keep your word, I must say. And I'm glad to hear you're not going to do things that I don't know anything about!"

"You'll keep it a secret then?" Kip gave her a swift hug. "Oh, Edna, you're a peach! I guess I was kind of silly, but gee, just think if I'd had a dog along, it would never have happened. I'll bet the dog would have saved me."

"You've no need to go getting yourself nearly drowned just to prove you need a dog, skipper," Edna said. "We know that already." She gave him a friendly cuff. "But I must say we haven't heard much about it lately, have we?"

Kip shrugged his shoulders. "What's the use of asking any more? I know Dad will never let me have one, and that's that." He brightened. "But Edna, maybe I'll get to know Dan better now."

"I hope so," Edna said. "That's an idea I'd like to promote after what he did for you today. Let me know if I can help."

"Nothing will help if I don't bump into him again soon," Kip said. "All I can do is hope."

6. Cave in the Mountain

"Too hot to work today," Mr. Mosely said. The following morning was sticky with the intense heat of mid-July. "We'll go to the mountain."

"I'd sure like that, Mr. Mosely," Kip said. "I've wanted to go there ever since you told us the legend." And to see the cave in the mountain, he added to himself, but he could manage that alone.

"Dan's father is doing some remodelling inside the restaurant," Mr. Mosely told him. "We'll be taking lumber up for him in the truck along with the plants."

Kip wondered if Mr. Stonefish had mentioned his silly accident at the Outlet to Mr. Mosely. But if the old man knew, he gave no sign.

They were soon on the highway, sharing the gumdrops that Albert had offered Kip on the way to work. The countryside simmered in the blaze of the morning. Picton, with its old houses set close on the street, was sheltered by towering maples.

Kip noticed the public library in the heart of the town and made a mental note to ask his father to take him there. Then he saw the Regent Theatre and wondered if he and Edna could go there sometime. Better still, suppose he and Dan could see a movie together one night? And have a sundae in the restaurant next door. His mother had never allowed him out at night at home, but after all, Dan was fourteen. Surely she would think it all right to be with him.

"We're nearly there," Mr. Mosely said. "The Bay's over on the left."

Kip saw the water, intensely blue in the morning light. He marvelled at the huge factory glistening on an enormous stone cliff.

"Cement plant," Mr. Mosely informed him. "We turn off just a piece up the road."

The long gradual incline to the mountain lake brought them to a cluster of small buildings and their journey's end.

"There's your lake." Mr. Mosely pointed. "You can look after yourself. I'll be busy with the owner inside." Kip was about to make off when his employer added shortly, "You'll have to help me carry these plants and the lumber in, of course."

"Oh, yes, of course, Mr. Mosely!" Kip felt foolish. In his excitement about the cave he had forgotten it was still a work day for him.

"Don't count on finding the cave." Mr. Mosely uncannily had read his mind. "The entrance to it is on private property down the road there." He disappeared into the restaurant without glancing back.

Kip felt a surge of disappointment. It was the cave he was counting on. A sudden anger against Mr. Mosely rose in him. Why did the old man seem to take pleasure in seeing his plans thwarted? It happened so many times. Then he remembered his father's words and the anger left him. That was Mr. Mosely and there was nothing he could do about it.

He walked quickly around the restaurant to the crest of the hill upon which it sat. A vast stretch of water, sparkling blue in the sunshine lay far below him. Long fingers of land pointing towards the west rode the blue expanse like a great green hand, waiting to lift the bay in its palm. As he searched for familiar landmarks he saw, in the far distance, the brown marsh grasses bordering Hay Bay, and he remembered with sudden pleasure the farm boy and the old church. He looked towards Adolphustown on the opposite shore. The car ferry, black and bulky against the clear water, was pulling out from the dock on its journey across the bay to Glenora. Much had happened since his father's car had made the same trip, new faces, new experiences, new possibilities. Then another possibility sprang to his mind. The hill was steep and dotted with tangled growth. He glanced down the quiet road to the house of which Mr. Mosely had spoken. The distance was not great. If the cave lay just below the house on the hill-side, why couldn't he try to reach it from the cliff? He took in the scene swiftly. He could hear the ring of a hammer up at the restaurant and the subdued roar of a power mower in the little park on the lake. There was no one in sight. Immediately he scrambled over the wooden fence that bordered the picnic ground where he had been standing.

The long grasses on the hill were slippery but he clung to the wiry bushes, hoping they would not give way. They came to an end and a wall of rock spread before him. Then he saw the hole. It was a narrow aperture about fifty feet from the top of the cliff. This must be the cave, but how was he to reach it? The sheer drop to the bay below was well over a hundred feet, and the distance to the cave entrance at least the length of his cottage's living-room. He looked down and saw a narrow path. It was not more than a foot wide but it led straight to the opening. As he thought of the Indians who might have used the trail in days long gone, of Englishmen and Frenchmen hiding from one another in the hot pursuit of battle, his excitement mounted. Without thinking further he left the safety of the trees and put one foot firmly on the path. Stone ledges jutted out at shoulder level and gave him something to cling to. His hands were wet with heat and excitement and he wiped them on his jeans one at a time. He proceeded with great caution, not daring to glance below. In a moment he crawled on to the ledge at the entrance to the cave and lay full length, his head just inside the opening. He felt triumphant. He had made it, and all alone, too! He raised his head and looked about him. The morning sun shone past him down a short passage that disappeared in darkness. He crawled along on all fours towards a single ray of light that lit up the blackness before him. He found that it shone into a small room where he could stand upright. It was a perfect hide-out, a fortress of rock not more than eight feet across. Against one wall an enormous rock was wedged tight and the beam of light was escaping from a tiny opening in the rock's side. The noise of a small stone tumbling down the face of the cliff came abruptly and startled him. A feeling of uneasiness enveloped him. It was kind of scary in this rock-bound room with its strange semi-twilight. He felt suddenly as if the ghosts of a dozen Frenchmen were staring at him from the nooks and crannies of the stone. He knelt down to crawl through the corridor. It would be good to feel the warmth and sun of the July morning. Then he stopped short. He realized with a jolt that there was no light at the end of the tunnel. But why? There had not been a cloud in the sky a few minutes ago. Without thinking he stood up and his head hit the tunnel roof with a crack.

"Ouch!" he cried out.

"What's the matter? Did you hurt yourself?"

Kip forgot the pain in his head at once. It was Dan's voice! "Dan!" he shouted.

"I'm out here on the ledge, waiting for you! Come and join me!"

Kip crawled to the cave's opening. "Hi!" he said. "How did you know I was here?"

"I saw you get out of the truck," Dan said, "and come down the hill. When I couldn't see you any more, I told Dad where I was going and followed you here."

"Didn't you think I'd make it?" Kip asked, grinning.

"Sure, but it's kind of tough going on the edge of the cliff if you're not used to it, especially after what happened . . ." Dan stopped.

"After what happened yesterday at the Outlet." Kip finished for him. "I know. I was one great big silly down there. But honestly, I do know how to swim. It was just that my mouth was full of water."

"You've got to be prepared for emergencies like that," Dan said. "Have you been swimming for long?"

"Pretty long. We had a cottage up north and I used to swim there, but I can't do the crawl. I can't seem to breathe right."

"I'd like to teach you," Dan said.

"You would?" Kip stared at him, unbelieving. All these weeks he had dreamed of friendship with Dan, and there it was, as simple as that. "Gee, I'd like that a lot!"

"It's a bargain," Dan said. "When do you want your first lesson?"

"As soon as you can give it to me."

"Good. Shall we make it Monday right after lunch? Dad will be finished up here by then, and he can take us down to our own cabin."

"Where shall I meet you?" Kip asked.

"At the store."

"I'll be there!" Kip knew he would have to convince his mother but he would get Edna on his side first.

Dan stood up on the ledge. "We'd better get back now. Mr. Mosely will be worrying about you."

Kip couldn't imagine Mr. Mosely worrying about anybody,

but he rose to his feet. He looked down the mountain side as he did so. Quickly he turned and clung to the ledge, closing his eyes.

Dan smiled. "It's a long way down but don't let it worry you. Take it one step at a time going back and everything will be okay."

Kip felt foolish. "It just made me feel kind of dizzy for a minute," he said. "I never looked down at all on the way here."

"Here," Dan said, "hang on to me and look down gradually. Start with the rock you're sitting on and look down the face of the cliff until your eyes reach the water. You'll be okay then."

Kip did as he was told. Dan was talking softly all the while. "There's a story about this cave. Away back in the war between France and England when Kingston was Fort Frontenac, a French admiral hid up here to watch a battle between French and English men o' war down there in the bay."

It was not hard to imagine him, in cocked hat and sword, his beribboned wig askew after the long hard climb up the face of the cliff, peering from the hole in the stone.

"There's another story, too," Dan added, "that there's a room sealed off in this cave where the Frenchman hid his treasure."

More treasure! Kip turned to him eagerly. "I saw a big rock in there rolled up against the wall and there was light coming in."

"Yes, the owner of the house put that there so that the children wouldn't come to the cave. It could be pretty dangerous for them." Dan looked at Kip. "You're all right now, aren't you?"

"Sure. I'll make it all right."

"I'll go first," Dan said, "and look straight ahead."

It seemed only a second until their footing was firm.

Mr. Mosely was standing by the truck door when they came

over the crest of the hill. "It's time you came," he said. "I've been waiting."

"I'm sorry," Kip said. "I didn't mean to be so long."

Dan made off towards the restaurant. "See you Monday!" he called. "Don't forget!"

Forget? How could he forget? Even Mr. Mosely's annoyance could not dampen his spirits. "I got to the cave after all," he said proudly, "and Dan met me there."

"Is that where you were?" Mr. Mosely gave him a quick glance. "How did you get down there?"

"Along the edge of the cliff," Kip said. "It wasn't really so hard. But I really am sorry I kept you waiting. I just remembered we have a man coming about some plants, haven't we?"

"Yes, but he can wait, too." Kip was relieved at the mild tone. He must remember not to keep Mr. Mosely waiting again.

Dan and the visit to the cave were the sole topics of his conversation when he arrived home. He carefully skipped the details as to how the cave was reached, knowing what his mother's reaction would be. He was wondering how he could broach the matter of the swimming lessons when Edna put a dish before him. "Humph," she remarked. "Much use it is making your favourite dessert. Not so much as a smile or a thank you for it."

"Chocolate pie!" he said. "Oh, boy, Edna! It looks super!"

"Too bad your father isn't here," Mrs. Brooks said. "It's his favourite, too."

Yes, it was too bad, Kip thought, because he could ask him about the swimming lessons. But what would be the use? It was his mother he had to convince, anyway. "Mom," he said quickly, "you know how much I want to learn the crawl, don't you?"

"Yes," his mother said, "but that doesn't seem to have much to do with chocolate pie."

Kip smiled. "I know it doesn't. It's just that Dan offered to teach me today. Isn't that great?"

Edna looked up. His mother's face brightened. "Why, I think that's wonderful, dear. When is he coming?"

"That's just it, Mom," Kip said. "He wants me to go to his father's cabin. I think he wants his father to watch out for us while we're having the lesson." Dan had not said so but it made it all sound so much safer.

His mother frowned. "Oh, I don't know about that, Kip."

"Oh, please, Mom!" It was so important that he get away with his new friend. He did not want their friendship to begin here where his mother would be watching over him like a baby. "I'll be careful, Mom. I won't do a thing I shouldn't."

He caught Edna's shrewd gaze and knew that she was thinking of the Outlet. "Anyway, I'll bet Mr. Stonefish will be there all the time to look after us."

"We should meet these people before you go off with them," Mrs. Brooks said. "I'll speak to your father about it when he comes down." And that was all she would say.

Mr. Brooks arrived on Friday at sunset. Kip, Edna and Mrs. Brooks were sitting on the beach after a swim, watching the liquid path of light from horizon to shore. Kip half closed his eyes and saw two boys, one dark-skinned and older than the other, floating in a canoe along the golden trail towards the Sandbanks and the sun. Then he heard the car in the lane and leaped up to greet his father.

"Hi, Dad!" he shouted. "I have something to ask you. Something terribly important!"

"For goodness' sakes," Edna exclaimed. "Let your poor father get his breath, will you?"

"Yes, at least here I can get one," Mr. Brooks laughed. "Whew! It's been a terrible week in the city. You three people don't know how lucky you are!"

"We've been thinking of you in all this heat," Mrs. Brooks said. "Are you going in for a swim?"

"As soon as I can change!" Mr. Brooks said.

"But that's what I have to ask you, Dad," Kip broke in. "It's about Dan and swimming lessons." He poured out his story. "Can I go, Dad? It would be super if I could learn the crawl."

"I think we'd better meet the young man first," Mr. Brooks said.

"Just what I said," Kip's mother put in.

"But how shall we do that before Monday?" Kip asked angrily. "I have to meet him at the store!"

"We'll see," Mr. Brooks said. "Now does anybody want to come in with me?"

Kip tried to stifle his annoyance. "Sure, I'll come, Dad," he said, "but you won't forget I want to know about Dan, will you?"

"You'd hardly let me," his father said, laughing.

"Kip should have a friend here," Mrs. Brooks said. "And that Indian boy did look like a fine lad."

Kip could have hugged her. "Then I can go?" he said.

"We'll see what tomorrow brings," his father told him. "Who'd like to come fishing with me in the morning, early?"

"I would!" Kip jumped up. "Then maybe after we could go and find Dan!"

"We'll have Edna fix us up a lunch right after breakfast," Mr. Brooks decided. Then he went to find his bathing-suit.

At breakfast the next morning Mrs. Brooks sighed. "My, oh my! What a shame I've never learned to fish!"

"Gosh, Mom!" Kip said. "If you really want to learn, I'll teach you!"

"You will?" Mrs. Brooks looked delighted. "Pack up another lunch, Edna. I'm on my way already!"

Out on the water, as they drifted into a quiet cove deeper than their own, Mrs. Brooks rose suddenly in the small row-boat. "There's something on the line," she cried. "I can feel it tugging!"

"Better sit down, Bet," Mr. Brooks advised, "or we'll be fishing you out of the water!"

In a moment he had helped her land a good-sized fish. "A pickerel!" Kip shouted. "Mom, you got a fish!"

"May I try again? That was so easy! I'd love to try it once more, Allan!"

Mr. Brooks winked at Kip. "Somehow, I don't think you and I are going to get the feel of this rod much today, Kip," he said. "We'll let Mother catch all the fish and have a fish fry on the beach tonight."

But Mrs. Brooks was gazing up the long reaches of the narrow cove. "There are two people fishing up there," she said. "Aren't they waving at us?"

"Dan and his father!" Kip exclaimed. "Hurrah! Now you can meet Dan and make all the plans for Monday."

The introductions took only a moment when the two boats had met. "I understand you want to make a champion swimmer out of our boy, Dan," Mr. Brooks said.

"Not quite that," Dan grinned. "But I could teach him the crawl and a little more safety in the water."

Kip drew a sharp breath. He had forgotten that Dan might mention the Outlet incident. He was relieved when Mr. Stonefish broke in. "I'll be watching out for them until your son knows what he's doing," he said. "That's our cabin up at the head of the cove."

"You're sure he'll be all right?" Mrs. Brooks said anxiously. "The water here seems very deep."

"Oh, Mom!" Kip put in. "Of course I'll be all right. I'm not a baby!"

"It's not as deep close in to shore, Mrs. Brooks," Dan assured her. "I won't let him get in over his head until Dad says he's ready."

"Gosh," Kip said in disgust. "You'd think I couldn't swim at all!" Then he remembered the Outlet again and was silent.

"We certainly appreciate your doing this for Kip," Mr. Brooks said.

"Yes, I hope you'll come and see us at Kip's Cove soon, Dan," Mrs. Brooks added. "Perhaps you could teach me a thing or two."

"Me, too!" Kip's father sang out. "We could make it a real family swimming lesson and have Edna join us."

It was Edna who greeted them with approval as they rowed into the beach with five fish in mid-afternoon. "Coming up, one frying-pan and one gallon of sunburn lotion!" Edna said.

"How about a nice soft bed?" Kip called. "That rowing is hard work after six hours."

Later, on the beach, the fish sizzled in the pan and potatoes roasted in their jackets among the hot coals. They all jumped when one of them burst its skin. "Indians on the trail!" Mr. Brooks laughed.

Kip remembered Dan and wished that he were there. But then, Monday would not be long in coming and he would have Dan all to himself.

"Pity we couldn't eat this way every night," Edna said. "I'm going to need more time to myself if I'm going to have gentlemen callers first thing in the morning."

Mrs. Brooks looked puzzled. "Gentlemen callers?"

"Albert dropped in on me this morning," Edna explained. "We had a nice chat together, too."

"Albert?" It was Kip's turn to be puzzled. "What did he want?"

Edna spoke with mock seriousness. "Why, to spend an hour or two in my company I suppose. What else? He certainly enjoyed the coffee and muffins I gave him. I think he'll be back."

"Oh, Edna," Kip laughed. "You know Albert's never met you before! Why would he come and see you this morning?"

"Well, as a matter of fact, I wasn't the only person he came to see," Edna confessed. "He came to tell you he's got a new mail route and he'll be past an hour later in the mornings, and he won't be coming back home until late afternoon."

"Perfect!" Kip crowed. "That means Dan and I can swim every day and Mr. Stonefish won't have to bring me home!" Good old Albert! Everything was working out and now he could hardly wait for Monday to come.

7. Swimming Lessons and Tales of the Mohawks

The day arrived at last with a blazing sun in a clear sky. "Wonderful swimming weather," thought Kip as he waited for Albert.

"Makin' a lazy man of you," Albert commented. "Should make you get up at sunup and bike to work yourself."

"I guess I could do it if I had to," Kip said.

"Miss your company," Albert said. "Better stick with me." He rolled down the window to let in the fresh breeze off the lake. "Nice girl you've got workin' at your house."

"Edna?" Kip said. "Sure, she's super." He grinned. "She makes pretty good muffins, doesn't she?"

"Nothing much wrong with a woman who makes muffins like that," Albert admitted. He cast a long glance towards Kip. "Married?" he asked.

"Oh, no," Kip laughed. "I can't imagine Edna getting married. She's pretty old. I think I heard Dad say once she was thirty-three. Anyway, we couldn't get along without Edna. She'd never leave us to get married."

"Wouldn't, eh?" Albert said. "Pity. Nice girl."

But Kip was too intent on the afternoon to come to discuss Edna. All he wanted was to have the morning's work done and be on his way to the store. There, Mr. Stonefish's old car was already waiting for him although he was fifteen minutes early.

"Hi, Champ!" Dan called. "I hope you ate a good lunch. I'm going to work you pretty hard today!"

"I'm all ready for it," Kip said. "I can hardly wait."

On the way to the cove Kip sat in the back seat watching Mr. Stonefish's face in the rear-view mirror. He and Dan resembled one another closely, the same high cheek-bones and long thin features, both with heavily arched eyebrows and dark eyes. But Mr. Stonefish's skin was lighter than Dan's, a pale golden hue that could almost be mistaken for a coat of tan. Kip wondered why, when they were both of Indian blood.

The small cabin on the shore was almost hidden by trailing willows. "Dad and I stay here lots of times when he has summer work down here," Dan explained. "But it isn't big enough for Mom and the other kids as well."

"We're working on that." Mr. Stonefish pointed to some lumber in the rear of the cottage. "We'll get it into shape one day."

"I guess we forgot to tell you," Dan put in. "I have a younger brother and sister at home. Nina's six and Tom's eight. Our real home is up on the Reserve."

They were all ready for the water in a moment. "Let's fool around for a while first," Dan said. "Then we'll start with the lessons."

"You know one thing I've never liked to do?" Kip shouted. "Open my eyes under water!"

"That's where we start then," Dan said. "Come on! We'll do it together and go for Dad's legs."

Kip could not believe that an hour and a half could pass so quickly. By the end of it they had him floating face down in the water, eyes open and arms flailing out like some water windmill. "Boy! I think I'm getting it," he gasped, "but the breathing's the hardest, isn't it?"

"Not a bit, if you do what Dan tells you," said Mr. Stonefish. "I think you'd better plan on a lesson every day for a while until we know you can take care of yourself."

"There's nothing I'd like better," said Kip, and he wondered how he could be so lucky.

"Zowie! What a day!" he shouted, as he bounced into his own cottage in the late afternoon.

His mother was out on the verandah with Edna. She sprang to her feet. "Oh, Kip," she said, "I've been thinking of you all day. How did everything go?"

"Terrific!" Kip boasted. "I can practically do the crawl already."

"Sure," Edna said with a wry smile. "We'll announce that you're swimming the English Channel tomorrow."

"There is one thing to remember," Mrs. Brooks reminded him. "Your father's starting his holidays a week from Wednesday. We'd like you home for a while then, so that we can all have fun together."

"You mean I won't be able to work at the greenhouse any more?" Kip felt a pang of disappointment. He would miss Mr. Mosely, despite the old man's crustiness, and what would he do about Dan? Nothing must stand in the way of their relationship now that it was just beginning.

"Your father has explained things to Mr. Mosely, Kip," his mother said. "He thinks he can get along without you now. Most of his heavy work is done."

"But what about Dan?" Kip burst out.

"You should be well along with your lessons by then," Mrs. Brooks said, "and you'll have to have Dan over here some time."

But some time isn't enough, Kip thought. And yet he wanted to enjoy the family outings, too. Besides, his father was counting on him to go fishing and swimming. But the summer was so short, and Dan was his best friend now. He did not know what to do.

"Albert will miss you driving up and back," Edna was saying. "By the way, I've made a few extra muffins for his lunch. You can give them to him tomorrow morning. It's the least we can do when he's so good to you."

"He'll love that," Kip said. "He said you're a pretty good muffin maker."

"He did?" Edna smiled. "I'll make him an extra half dozen. A man always eats more when he doesn't get good home cooking."

By Thursday Kip was doing the crawl if not with finesse at least with confidence. "How am I doing?" he gasped after an especially long swim.

"So well, that if I took you over to the Outlet and threw you in the hole, I wouldn't give you a second thought," laughed Dan. "Come on up to the beach and have a rest. Mom stuck some cookies in my bag today."

They lay sprawled in the hot sand, drinking in the intense heat of the sun and enjoying the cookies. Kip heard the gentle wash of the waves on the shore and the far-off cry of a seagull winging in over the land. He was aware of Dan's lean brown figure beside him. He thought he had never been so happy in his life. Suddenly Dan's dog who had been lying asleep under the willows, swooped down on them.

"Oh, so you want to play, do you?" Kip shouted, and he rolled over and over in the sand with Tad. He sat up and hugged the dog to him. "Oh, Tad," he said, "I wish you belonged to me. You must be the best dog anybody ever had!"

"He is," Dan grinned, "but that's probably because he's mine. Why don't you borrow him for a day or two some time? I wouldn't mind."

Kip stroked the brown coat slowly. "I don't think they'd let me at home," he said. "They don't want me to have a dog.

But I can pretend he's mine while I'm here, can't I? Come on, Tad, I'll beat you to the willows and back!"

Boy and dog flopped on the sand, breathless, at the end of the run. "Dan," Kip said, "do you mind if I ask you a question?"

"Not if I can answer it," Dan said. "Don't put me on the spot."

"Is your father a real Indian?"

Dan sat up. "You mean because his skin isn't dark like mine?"

"Yes, that's why I asked."

"The reason for that goes back a long way," Dan said. "We're really related to an English nobleman, Sir William Johnson."

"An English nobleman!" Kip sat up, too. "Where did he come from?"

"He lived in the time of George the Third of England," Dan said, "about seventeen hundred and sixty, when England still ruled the American colonies. William Johnson was kind of the King's deputy in New England."

"How did he get to be related to the Indians?" Kip asked.

"As Mother tells the story, he liked the Indians and wanted to live with them in the Mohawk Valley, so he set up a trading-post there."

Kip moved back into the shade of a tree. Now that his body was dry the sun was too hot. "Where's the Mohawk Valley?" he asked.

"In the United States. It runs through New York State along the bed of the Mohawk River. That's where our Indian tribe got its name, The Mohawk. Sir William Johnson did a lot of fighting in the French and Indian wars. He was on the side of the English, of course, and his Indian friends fought with him. He even fought beside Wolfe on the Plains of Abraham and the Chief of the Six Nations gave him his own war-club for his courage."

"But you said he had something to do with your own family," Kip said.

"He did. Sir William married an Indian girl named Molly Brant. They had a daughter who married my father's great-grandfather. When the Americans began their revolution against the British, the Mohawks in the valley still wanted to stay under British rule, so they began to move up the river and into Canada with the United Empire Loyalists. My great-grandfather came with them as an overseer, but their chief commander was Molly Brant's brother, Joseph Brant." Dan smiled. "In Indian, Thayendinaga."

"But that's the name of your Reserve," Kip said. "I saw it on a sign when we came through Deseronto."

"That's right," said Dan. "It's an Indian word meaning crossed sticks. But Thayendinaga, or Joseph Brant, didn't come to the land where our Reserve is now. He went to land around Brantford to settle there. Part of the Indian band who came with him left his leadership and followed his cousin, John Deserontyou, to land on the Bay of Quinte."

"So that's where the other name comes from! Deseronto!" Kip said. "Your people were really United Empire Loyalists, too, just like the man Edna told me about in her ghost story."

"Yes, they were." Dan leaped up suddenly. "Let's not talk any more. Let's do something."

"What?" Kip jumped up, too, and the dog bounded to his side. "Come on, Tad, I'll race you in the water out to the log!"

"I thought we'd take the canoe out this time, Kip. Do you know how to paddle?"

Kip's face fell. "No, I don't. We only had a power boat up north."

"I'll teach you," Dan said. "Come on and help me get her down to the water. She's up behind the cabin."

After the row-boat, the canoe seemed very tippy to Kip. He could tell that it was very old, too, from the number of cracks and patches on its framework.

"We won't go too far from shore," Dan said, "until you've got the crawl perfect."

Dan made him move up to the bow while he gave the canoe a strong shove and leaped into the stern. He began paddling at once, keeping the canoe close to the shore.

"Don't sit on the thwart, Kip," said Dan. "Kneel on the cushion in front of you and lean back against the thwart. Now pick up your paddle and I'll set you to work."

He explained the three types of paddling to Kip, the forward or cruising stroke, the draw or turning stroke and the jam or stopping stroke.

"Now, before you start, turn round slowly and see how I'm holding my paddle, and you do the same."

Kip did as he was told, watching one of Dan's hands grasping the grip at the top of the paddle, and the other sliding down the shaft of the paddle to the throat just above the blade. "This upper hand does the driving," Dan explained, "with your arm close to your body. Be sure you put all the weight of your shoulder and body behind it."

When Dan had showed him the bow stroke, Kip tried it, feeling the water tug at his paddle blade. "I did it!" he shouted. "It's not so hard!"

"Of course it isn't," Dan laughed. "Now just keep doing that and we'll go for a trip along the shore."

How often Kip had envied Speedy Ashton his tales of canoe trips with the Scouts, and here he was, paddling a canoe himself, and with an Indian in the stern! If only Speedy and the others, John and Peter, Mike and Brian, could see him!

"Rest now!" Dan commanded, and they laid their paddles across the gunwales while the canoe drifted on the gentle swell towards the beach.

"Can't I paddle where you are?" Kip asked.

"I'll teach you that on Monday when you've had more practice in the bow," Dan promised.

"Couldn't we do it tomorrow?" Kip said. "I don't want to have to wait the whole week-end!"

"We'll see how you do with the swimming, Champ," Dan said. "I think we've nearly got that under control."

On Friday Kip made such a determined effort that Dan agreed to an hour in the canoe. Kip wondered as he paddled proudly in the stern, what he could ever do to repay Dan. He had the money he had earned at the greenhouse. He had been hoarding every penny in an old tobacco tin of his father's, hoping that if he put it before his parents at the right time, they would consent to a dog. But all the giving could not be on one side, and Dan had given him so much. What could he buy with twenty dollars? Sometimes they sold transistor radios for twenty dollars. He saw them in the paper. But Dan had never mentioned one of those. Perhaps he didn't listen to the radio much.

"There's another leak up here in the bow," Dan was saying. "We'll have to do a patching job this afternoon."

That was it! Why had he not thought of it before? He would buy Dan a new canoe! But canoes cost much more than twenty dollars, and he was leaving the work at the greenhouse next week. He would figure out a way somehow. He just had to. A canoe of his very own for Dan. That was certainly the answer.

Clouds were thickening in the sky as they beached the canoe, and when the patching job was done, the first few drops of rain fell.

"Let's go into the cabin and wait for Dad," Dan suggested. He gathered some driftwood and carried it inside. "This place has been shut up, so we'll build a fire to take away the musty smell."

Kip admired his friend's skill at the stove. It was obvious that he had tended many fires, but then, it seemed to Kip that Dan did everything well.

As they squatted cobbler fashion on the braided rug in front of the stove, Kip thought, "It's just like a camp-fire. Dan and I are out on a canoe trip and we're camping here for the night." Then the dog came and put his head in Kip's lap and he rubbed his ears gently. "Nice old thing," he said. "Good old dog."

"Dad and I were wondering if you would come up to the Reserve with us on Monday, instead of coming here," Dan said suddenly.

"To Deseronto?" Kip sat up straight. "Boy, would I love that! But would they let me on the Reserve when I'm not an Indian?"

"Sure. We've been telling Mom and Nina and Tom about you, and they'd like to meet you, that is if your mother will let you come."

"Oh, she'll let me, I know she will!" He really knew nothing of the sort, but this wouldn't stand in the way of his persuading her!

"We'd like you to come for lunch if Mr. Mosely will let you off early," Dan said. "I thought we'd take you over to see Len Big Canoe in the afternoon. Maybe he'll tell you some of his Indian stories."

"Len Big Canoe?" Kip repeated. "Who is he?"

"The oldest man on the Reserve. He knows lots of legends. You might have a hard time to understand him. You see, lots of older people on the Reserve can't read or write."

Kip looked puzzled. "But you have schools there. Mr. Mosely told us your father and mother are both teachers."

Dan nodded. "Yes, but it wasn't always like that. Some of the very old folks haven't been to school at all. Now the boys and girls on the Reserve have to go to school until they're sixteen, and some even go on to university. Old Len talks English, you know, but he's a bit slow sometimes, that's all."

He found his mother and Edna playing Scrabble in the cedar grove when he got home. He burst out at once with the news of the Reserve visit. "I can go, can't I, Mom?" he said. "I may never ever get another chance to go on a Reserve!"

"I suppose that's true," Mrs. Brooks smiled. "It's all right with me. We'll ask your Dad when he comes tonight."

"I don't know what's the matter with us," Edna grumbled. "You never want to stay around home any more. We'd like a little company ourselves, you know."

Kip flopped beside her on one of the old desks. "But I'm home every day at four, Edna, and we all go in swimming together then, and after supper, too. Come on, I'll go you a game of Scrabble now, both of you!"

"I hope your father comes early enough for a swim tonight," Mrs. Brooks said. "We'll wait for him, anyway."

But he had not arrived by sunset and they swam while there was still light in the sky. "Wouldn't you know he'd be late tonight," Kip thought. "Just when I wanted to ask him about the Reserve."

"You mustn't wait up any longer," Mrs. Brooks said at ten. "He's been held up by a client, I expect. Off to bed now and you can have a chat with him first thing tomorrow morning."

Kip was up with the sun, searching for shells in the wet sand. The sky was clear and the air fresh and cool after Friday's brief rain. His parents were not stirring when he left the cottage and he wandered alone up the beach, wondering if he dared ask his father, too, about having Dan's dog for a few days.

"What's all this I hear about a reserve?"

Kip turned at the sound of his father's voice. "I didn't know you were up yet," he said.

"No use staying in bed with all this to enjoy," Mr. Brooks said. "I'm counting on a swim before breakfast."

"Can I go, Dad? To the Reserve, I mean?"

"I can't see anything against it," Mr. Brooks said. "But aren't you ever going to invite that boy here? We'd like to see something of him, too, you know, Kip."

"Some time, maybe," Kip said, but he promised himself it would not be for a while. He liked being off alone with Dan.

He didn't have his mother or Edna worrying about him there, and Dan treated him man to man.

"How about a walk up the creek?" Mr. Brooks suggested. "Are you game?"

"Sure!" said Kip, following him.

Here, in the strange daylight gloaming of the woods, they could hear the strident shout of a bluejay over their heads. All the minute sounds of the forest were around them in the still of the morning.

"You know," said Mr. Brooks, "this should be an excellent place to dig for Indian relics. Didn't Mr. Mosely tell us it used to be an Indian trail in the old days?"

"That's what he said," Kip agreed. "Let's dig, Dad! Maybe I could find an arrowhead to show Dan."

"Fetch the spade from the tool-shed," Mr. Brooks said, "and we'll go up to the clearing to see what we can find."

They worked their way through underbrush up the creek until they came to the small pond. It was deep and quiet, with only water-spiders spinning across its surface like miniature surf-board riders.

"This would be a good place to start," Mr. Brooks said.

"A good place for what?"

They wheeled, startled, to find Kip's mother peering at them through the bushes. "Don't look so surprised," she smiled. "Edna says breakfast is nearly ready and she doesn't want the bacon to spoil." When they told her about the digging she added, "Well, if you're looking for treasure, I'm coming, too!"

They all returned to the pond after breakfast. "If there's going to be a find," Edna said firmly, "the dishes can wait."

For two hours they dug, carefully examining every lump of sod. "I don't think the Indians were even ever here!" Kip said in disgust. "All I've found is a nest of nuts some old squirrel left!"

"Wait a minute, what's this?" Mrs. Brooks called. She was kneeling on the springy earth on the other side of the pond.

"What's what?" Kip was beside her in an instant. "Dad, look! Mom's found something!"

"By George! Bet, I think it's an arrowhead, all right." Mr. Brooks examined the small object she handed him. "I told you we'd find something here!"

"Boy, Mom, you're smart! First the fish and now this!" Kip said. "Can I hold it for a minute?" He turned the triangular stone chip over and over, wondering what hands had held it before him. Perhaps they might have belonged to a young boy like himself, or to a brave Indian chief going forth to do battle with a neighbouring tribe. The arrowhead brought to him a vision of Indian tepees set up in a circle around a blazing camp-fire on this very spot and the beat of tom-toms resounding through the forest. "Gosh," he said finally, "if we never find anything else, this was worth all the digging."

"Spoken like a true archaeologist," Mr. Brooks said, clapping him on the back.

"And speaking of digging," Edna said, "if I don't dig those dishes out of the sink, I'll never be finished my work in time for the movie tonight."

"Movie?" Mrs. Brooks sounded surprised. "You're going out, Edna?"

"Albert's taking me to Picton," Edna said. "He likes Westerns, so I'll likely be riding the range all night."

"Zowie! Can I come, Edna? I love Westerns, too!" Kip said.

"Of course you can't, Kip," Mr. Brooks put in quickly. "This is Edna's night out. She doesn't want you along."

Kip felt a sudden twinge of jealousy. He and Edna had always done things together before. He did not want even Albert interfering.

"Cheer up, skipper," Edna smiled. "I'll tell you the whole plot tomorrow, and I won't leave out a single shot!"

On Sunday, her enthusiasm for Albert's company was quite evident. Kip wondered if Albert had enjoyed the evening half as much. Secretly he hoped that he had not. He could not share Edna with anyone, even for the summer. But he could not begrudge her a little entertainment. After all, he was going to spend a whole day on the Reserve with Dan, and the way the summer was going, just anything could happen.

8. A Day with the Indians

"Dan wants me to go to the Reserve for lunch today, Mr. Mosely," Kip said on Monday, even before he was inside the greenhouse door. "Can I get off early?"

Mr. Mosely did not bother to look at him. "I was counting on getting some transplanting done today," he grumbled.

"I'll work twice as hard tomorrow," Kip promised. "I'll stay overtime if you want me to."

"That won't be necessary. You can go," said Mr. Mosely. "They tell me you won't be here much longer, anyway."

"No, I'm sorry, Mr. Mosely." Kip went up to the old man. "I'll really miss it here. I like the greenhouse and I . . . well . . . I want to say thank you for having me."

"Not much use saying thank you when you don't intend to stay," said Mr. Mosely.

"But I'd stay if my father wasn't having his holidays, Mr. Mosely, honestly I would."

"Maybe." Mr. Mosely gave a curt nod. "You can start to

112

work over on the zinnias. We don't get anything done by talk."

Kip felt deflated but he could not be unhappy for long. Within two hours he was on his way to meet Dan and his father at the store. Mr. Bell was sitting on the verandah fanning himself with an old newspaper. "Whew!" he said. "What's up, Chris? You look as if you were on your way to a bargain sale."

"I'm meeting Dan here, Mr. Bell," Kip puffed. "His father's taking me down to the Reserve today, isn't that great?"

"I should say," Mr. Bell agreed. "Haven't even been there myself, in all the years I've lived here. Tell me what it's like tomorrow, eh?"

"Sure! Look, here they come now. I just made it on time!"

They were soon on their way. On the outskirts of Picton they passed a plain white frame building standing with quiet dignity beneath a huge old elm tree. "That place should interest you," Mr. Stonefish remarked. "It's called the White Chapel. It was built in the year 1809."

Kip remembered the church on the road to Hay Bay, the very beginning of his summer adventures. "What's it like inside?" he asked.

Dan described it.

"Just like my church," Kip said, and he told them about Hay Bay.

The highway ran beside Picton Bay for a great part of the journey, and then along the sparkling waters of Long Reach. Rich pasture land rolled up from the opposite shore, dotted with prosperous farms. The pavement ended suddenly and they were on a bumpy road, winding and narrow. As they broke over a steep hill, they saw the blue waters of the Bay of Quinte, and a small white shack boasting a STOP sign and the announcement of the ferry service. A crude dock awaited the car ferry, at that moment on its way towards them.

"That's the Reserve across the water," Dan said. "As soon

as we dock on the other side, we'll be there."

Kip gazed over the slim arm of water. A number of small houses nestled in the folds of the fields. A church spire towered in the distance beyond a grove of trees. But apart from a number of dark-haired children skipping up the lane, the scene was one of country quiet.

On board the ferry Mr. Stonefish pointed down the long splendid reaches of the bay to the westward. "This water is really an arm of Lake Ontario," he said, "that cuts the island of Quinte, or Prince Edward County as it's known on the map, off from the mainland. It goes on west there to a narrow neck of land joining the mainland and the island at Carrying Place."

"That's a funny name," Kip said. "Would it be called that because the Indians used to portage across it to the mainland?"

"That's exactly the reason," Dan said. "Look, we're coming in to land. Let's get back in the car."

As they drove off the ferry Dan turned to his father. "Where are we going to take him first, Dad?"

"Let's go to the landing place," Mr. Stonefish said. "That's as good a beginning as any."

A few moments later, after a drive through the village, they stopped on the highway before a large stone cairn in a grassy enclosure well back from the road. Kip followed his friends through the gate and read the inscription on the plaque of the cairn.

THE COMING OF THE MOHAWKS

"Commemorating the arrival here on the 22nd May, 1784, under the leadership of Chiefs John Deserontyou, Aaron and Isaac Hill, of a band of loyal Mohawks, one of the Nations of the Iroquois Confederacy, expelled from their home in the Mohawk Valley for their fidelity to the Unity of Empire."

"You might say this is where we began," Mr. Stonefish smiled. "Our great-grandfathers were in that band. But come along now, Mother and the children are probably out front watching for us."

"How big is the Reserve, anyway?" Kip asked as the car made a turn on the gravelled road.

"It's three miles up the Bay and ten miles along its shoreline," Dan said. "Our house is about five miles from here."

Nina and Tom were waiting at the gate when they arrived at the two-storey house. It was on a parcel of farm land with woods at its back door and a host of petunias trooping their gay colours behind the white picket fence. The children flung themselves on their father with a shout but ran back as Kip stepped out of the car. Mrs. Stonefish came from the side door of the house, her hand outstretched. She was of a heavier build than his own mother, with black hair coiled in a smooth bun, dark skin like her son's, and merry brown eyes.

"This is a fine day for us," she said rather shyly. "How nice of you to come and see us."

"It's very nice of you to have me here," Kip said stiffly, not yet at ease.

"Welcome to our wigwam," Mr. Stonefish smiled. "And you'd be surprised how many people think we still live in them!"

"I guess they're like me," Kip said. "I've never known any Indians before I met Dan and you. I didn't even know what a Reserve was like or anything."

Mrs. Stonefish eyed the two smaller children playing tag in and out of the front door. "As for wigwams," she said, "sometimes I think they might be a good idea."

They all laughed and followed her into the big kitchen. Nina and Tom soon forgot their shyness and ran back and forth from the toy box bringing their playthings for Kip's approval.

During lunch they talked about Indian tribes. "I know your tribe is called the Mohawk," Kip said, "but were they part of a larger tribe?"

"Part of the Iroquois," Mr. Stonefish told him. "The Iroquois were a group of tribes who spoke dialects of the same language. They lived for the most part by farming. They were made up of two groups; the Hurons, the Tobacco nation and the Neutrals were one; the second group that lived in the United States were the Seneca, the Cayuga, the Onondaga, the Oneida and the Mohawk. This second group organized itself into the League of Five Nations, which later became the League of Six Nations when another tribe joined."

Dan rose from the table. "Dad, we'd better be getting over to old Len's before he takes his afternoon sleep."

W. Wheeler

"He's very old, Kip," Mr. Stonefish said. "If he likes you he'll talk, if he doesn't he won't. Don't be disappointed if we can't get a story out of him."

Shortly after the car drew up at a very small house painted dark green. Under a large maple tree Len Big Canoe sat smoking a large black pipe. There was a dog beside him.

"You never told me he had a dog," Kip whispered. "A German Shepherd, too! He's a beauty!"

The dog sat up straight, ears pointing, as they approached. At a word from his master, he whined and lay down again.

"Hello, Len," Mr. Stonefish shouted. "We've brought a friend of Dan's to meet you today." He eased the way with questions about the old Indian's health and the weather. Then he suggested that Kip would like to hear the legend of the Five Nations.

The old man's smoky black eyes stared at Kip for a long moment. "I will tell this boy the story of Dekanawida," he said at last.

With short rhythmic sentences and thin flute-like voice, Len Big Canoe took Kip back to the time of longhouse and wigwam and birch bark canoe. He told the story of a proud Huron chief, Dekanawida, who wanted all men to live as brothers. Neither Hurons nor Mohawks would listen to his words of good will until a young Indian brave, Hiawatha, came to help him. Together they persuaded the Mohawks to join the Five Nations in a bond of friendship and peace. The League they began became a tool of wise government for all the Indian peoples in its organization, overcoming the jealousy and hatred that had led to constant warfare between the tribes.

"You might call it the first United Nations," Mr. Stonefish said when Len Big Canoe had finished.

Kip shook the old man's hand awkwardly. "Thank you for telling me the story, Mr. Big Canoe," he said. He knelt beside the chair. "I just love your dog," he added, and the big German Shepherd suddenly laid his head across Kip's knees.

"Old Len can't hear you," Dan said. "He's pretty deaf. But his dog sure knows what you're talking about."

Kip stroked the beautifully shaped head. "Gosh, what a dog! He's about the best-looking dog I've ever seen, and he's not mean. I've always heard that German Shepherds were mean."

"Old Len wouldn't have a mean dog," Mr. Stonefish smiled, "but if anybody came here that shouldn't, he could be mean enough, believe me. He knows you're his friend."

"Poor old thing." Dan stooped to pat him, too. "It's too bad about you, boy, but it just can't be helped."

"What do you mean?" Kip glanced up quickly. "What do you mean, too bad about him, Dan?"

"Oh, nothing." Kip saw Mr. Stonefish shake his head at Dan. "Come along now. Let's go along and see the Council Hall."

But Kip was wondering about Dan's words even while he was waving good-bye to the old man.

As they went a red car drew up at the gate. "There's Mr. Cassie coming to see old Len," Mr. Stonefish said. He turned to Kip. "He's the agent here, the government representative on the Reserve who has to look after just about everything."

"Everything from hiring new teachers to putting gravel on the Reserve roads," Dan laughed.

"You boys wait here," Mr. Stonefish said. "I want to have a word with him before he talks to old Len." And he went towards the jovial-faced man who was walking up the lane.

Kip faced Dan. "Dan, what did you mean, it's too bad about the dog? There's something wrong with him, isn't there?"

"No, not really." Dan glanced in his father's direction. "Len's son gave him this dog two years ago to keep him company, but Len has got too old to live alone any longer and he has to go up to Brantford to stay with his daughter."

"And what about the dog? Is he going, too?"

"That's just the trouble. The daughter already has a dog

and doesn't want him, and neither does anybody else."

Kip stared at him. "You mean nobody on the Reserve wants him either?"

"Most of us here have dogs, Kip," Dan said. "And a big dog like that is expensive to feed."

"But they couldn't . . . they wouldn't . . ." Kip could not finish the sentence.

"I don't know what they're going to do. They can't let him run around loose, that's for sure. Somebody'll have to take him in or he'll have to be done away with."

Done away with! Kip looked back at the dog, at the fine, intelligent face, and felt a lump swell in his throat. He turned away quickly and began to walk towards the road.

"Don't worry about it, Champ," Dan said. "Maybe somebody'll want him yet."

What a great fool he was making of himself, almost crying over a dog in front of Dan. He forced a smile as Mr. Stonefish approached and introduced the agent.

"And now we'll see the Council Hall," Mr. Stonefish said. "Sorry to keep you waiting."

Council Hall? Who cared about Council Halls when that beautiful dog was watching them go, the big dark eyes wide, the ears pointed, listening for a friendly word. But he must be polite. He was still visiting.

"What happens at the Council Hall?" Kip asked as they drew up before a large two-storey frame building. *Oh, if only they'd let me have a dog at home, he thought. Here's the perfect dog for me. Nobody wants him and he's the best dog I've ever seen.*

"The Indian Council meets here on the first Wednesday afternoon of every month," Mr. Stonefish explained. "Mr. Cassie attends the council meetings as the government agent but the Indians themselves look after the business of the Reserve. They deal with transfers of land from one family to another, with leases and bills that have to be paid. They try to help people in need and to iron out family arguments."

Family arguments. Would there be much of a family argument if he said he wanted the dog? Why didn't he ask old Len if he could buy the dog right now with his twenty dollars? If he took him home, surely nobody would make him send him away again, to be destroyed.

"If a white man wants to stay on the Reserve, he has to get permission from the council, too," Dan was saying, "and the request is brought up at the meeting."

"Can a white person buy land on your Reserve?" Kip asked. *No, he considered. That wasn't the right way to go about it. Perhaps he should phone his father from Mr. Bell's store and ask him. He could not wait till he came down. The dog might be gone. Yes, that's what he would do. He would phone his father.*

Mr. Stonefish shook his head. "No, Kip, he can't. He's allowed to lease land from an Indian but only after the Council has approved of it."

Kip was gazing at the circular enclosure behind the Council Hall. "That looks like a race track," he said.

"It is," Mr. Stonefish said. "The Indian fair, or Mohawk Fair as it's usually called, is held here every September."

"I hope you can come with us this year," Dan said. "There are all sorts of competitions going on, and booths selling all kinds of stuff. They have a big parade round the track and then horse races and foot races for the kids and adults."

"At night, after they've served a big supper in the hall, they clear the floor and have fiddlers' contests," Mr. Stonefish said. "The Mounted Police turn up in their scarlet uniforms, and so do other government representatives and merchants from town. On a good day we'll get about two thousand people. Indians come back for it from Buffalo, Rochester, and other places in Canada and the U.S., and this makes it like a huge family reunion."

"And I know somebody who's wondering where the family

is right now," Dan said, "and that's Mom! Let's go back, shall we?"

"Oh, I don't think I'd better stay too long," Kip said. "I don't want to miss Albert at the store." *And I just can't wait to call Dad, he thought. I just can't wait to see what he'll say.*

Dan looked disappointed. "I was counting on a hike in the bush," he said. "We'll take you home if you miss Albert."

"Okay." Kip could not let him down. There would still be time to phone his father. Surely no one would come to take the dog away today.

Later, they sat whittling astride a fallen tree in the bush. "This is a wonderful place to live," Kip said.

"I wish it was right on the lake," Dan said. "I love canoeing and I could get in lots more of it then. One day I'll have a new canoe of my own, a red one, I hope, with the name in silver on the prow."

"What would you call her?" Kip asked.

"Kanati. That means lucky hunter." Dan smiled. "I'm not counting on it for a while yet, Champ. We always need so many things at home, and Nina and Tom are always growing out of their clothes. But maybe, some day."

"What's the dog's name, Dan?"

"Are you still worrying about him?" Dan frowned. "I wish I hadn't told you now. His name is Scout."

Scout! Kip imagined himself racing along the beach shouting the name. *Scout! Scout!* He could almost feel the powerful body leaping up at him, the cold tongue on his face. *Dad just had to say yes! He just had to!*

They were on their way back to Bloomfield by three o'clock. As they approached the village, Kip spoke up. "Mr. Stonefish, would you mind if I stopped at Mr. Bell's store for a minute?"

"Not at all. Have you money with you to get what you need?"

"Yes, thank you." He bounded up Mr. Bell's steps two at a

time and into the store. The storekeeper was perched on his tall stool reading a newspaper. "Well, well," he said. "Nice to see you again, Chris. How are the holidays going?"

"Fine, thank you, Mr. Bell," Kip hesitated. "Mr. Bell, I wondered if I paid you now, could I make a long distance call on your phone?"

"Long distance call, eh?" Mr. Bell peered over his glasses. "Somebody in trouble?"

"No, I just want to talk to my dad. It's important, Mr. Bell. Could I, please?"

"Well, I suppose we can find out the charge later from the operator. I don't see why not. Do you know how to place the call?"

"I guess not." Kip picked up the receiver nervously. Now that the time had come he felt shaky all over. What would his father say?

"You tell me the number and I'll fix things up for you," Mr. Bell said.

In a moment the voice of his father's secretary came through clearly. "Is my father there, please?" Kip said.

"I beg your pardon."

"Is Mr. Brooks there, please? I want to speak to him."

"I'm sorry, he's just stepped out of the office for a minute."

Kip's heart sank. He felt for the money in his pocket. He would never have enough for two phone calls.

Then the girl spoke again. "Oh, hold on! Are you still there? He's just come in."

Kip heard his father's astonished voice answer him. "Kip! Is something the matter?"

"No, Dad. That is, not much is the matter. It's about a dog, Dad."

"A dog? You're calling me about a dog?"

Kip poured forth the story of Len Big Canoe and the German Shepherd. "And you know I've always wanted a dog, Dad. We can't let him be taken away. He's the best dog I've ever seen! Honestly, I'd look after him. I wouldn't let him be any trouble. Please, Dad! Please let me have him!"

There was such a long silence that Kip thought his father had hung up. "Dad!" he shouted. "Dad, are you still there?"

"I'm here." His father's voice was quiet. "You haven't spoken to your mother yet, have you?"

"No, I haven't had a chance. But she always says you have to say 'yes' or 'no', you know that." Kip felt the lump in his throat again.

"Well . . ."

Kip's heart was in his mouth.

"Why don't you ask your friend Mr. Stonefish to tell Mr. Big Canoe not to let the dog go until I can see him. I'll be up on Wednesday afternoon."

When he had hung up Kip turned to Mr. Bell with a shout. "He didn't say 'no', Mr. Bell, and I thought he would! He didn't say 'no' at all!" He tore out of the door and down to the car. "Dan! Mr. Stonefish!" he shouted. "Maybe I can have Scout! Dad says he's going to have a look at him! Maybe he'll be my own dog, if Mr. Big Canoe will let me have him!"

"Gosh!" Dan said, when he realized what Kip meant. "Old Len will be pretty pleased if your father will let you have Scout. That's why his daughter can't get him to go. He doesn't want anything to happen to the dog!"

"Zowie! I didn't pay Mr. Bell!" Kip raced back to the store.

As the car pulled to a stop in his own lane, he almost forgot, in his excitement, to say thank you for the visit. "That's all right," Mr. Stonefish said as he ran back. "I guess you want to tell your mother all about the dog."

"Oh, no!" said Kip. "I won't breathe a word to her, or to Edna. I'm going to let my dad do all the talking. But just the same, I can hardly wait till Wednesday!"

9. A Dog Named Scout and a Red Canoe

Wednesday was only two days away but Kip had never spent a longer two days in his life. A dozen times or more he was on the point of bursting out with the news. All the while he worked in the greenhouse he longed to tell Mr. Mosely, but thought it wiser to keep silent until he knew for sure. Instead, he talked about dogs in general, asking questions, telling stories about his friends' dogs until, on Wednesday morning, Mr. Mosely said, "Pity I didn't have a dog here. You might not leave the job if there was one around the greenhouse."

"But I liked working here, Mr. Mosely," Kip said. "I'll come back next summer, if you'll have me." Perhaps I'll bring my own dog with me then, he thought joyfully.

"Maybe." And Mr. Mosely fell silent. When it was time for Kip to go in mid-afternoon, he merely shook hands and said a curt thank you.

But Kip was too happy to be hurt. "Mr. Mosely, this may be the last day for me working here, but I'll come up and see you really soon again, and I know Mom would like you to come down and see us, too." He caught sight of a quick, pleased smile on the old man's face and then he heard his father's car on the road. "See you, Mr. Mosely! Thanks for everything!"

His father leaned out to greet Mr. Mosely, and then they drove off. "Do you know how to get to this place?" he asked.

"Sure I do. I know every bit of the way."

"Let's go then. But remember, I'm not promising anything," Mr. Brooks said. "It all depends on the dog."

"There's one thing for sure," Kip grinned, "if I had Scout you'd never have to worry about me getting into trouble again. He'd sure look after me all right."

"Getting into trouble?" Mr. Brooks glanced at him quickly. "What do you mean by that?"

"Oh, nothing." Kip realized too late that his father knew nothing about the Outlet incident. "I just mean trouble in the water or anything like that. A dog is a wonderful protector."

Mr. Brooks stopped the car abruptly. "Have you been in some trouble that you haven't told us about? You said, 'again'!"

Kip's cheeks burned. "Oh, gosh, I didn't mean to say anything about it. It wasn't much, anyway. I just couldn't breathe because my mouth was full of water." He told the story quickly, not looking at his father.

When he had finished, Mr. Brooks frowned. "Kip, that boy and his father saved your life and you never gave your mother and me the opportunity to express our gratitude?"

"Well, if I'd told Mom, she'd never have let me go away again, you know that! Edna knew, anyway!"

"Well, that makes it a little better." Mr. Brooks started the car. "What in the world are we going to do for Dan to say 'thank you'?"

Kip said, "I know something I'd get for him if I had enough money."

"What's that?"

"A red canoe of his very own. That's what he wants more than anything. And he'd call it Kanati. That means lucky hunter in Indian."

"But they already have a canoe," Mr. Brooks said. "You told me he was teaching you to paddle it."

"Oh, it's only an old one," Kip said. "It's all holes and patches. I have twenty dollars, Dad, but if I spend that on the dog, I'll have to start saving up for the canoe all over again."

Mr. Brooks smiled. "At least we can invite him down to the cottage. Let's make a beginning there and we may think of something else later on."

When they arrived at the Stonefish house, Dan and his father were cutting dead branches from a pine tree. Mr. Brooks strode out to meet them. "I understand that you have some very late words of thanks coming to you, Dan," he said. "Kip here was a little tardy in telling us all about it."

"Words of thanks?" Dan looked puzzled.

"About what happened at the Outlet," Kip broke in. "I just told Dad now."

Dan grinned, embarrassed. "Oh, that was nothing, Mr. Brooks."

Mr. Stonefish joined them. "It'll never happen again, anyway. The way your boy is swimming now he could rescue somebody himself!"

"I still think it was a very great deal, and a mere thank you seems hardly enough," Mr. Brooks said gravely. "Would you come over and spend Saturday and Sunday with us?"

Dan glanced at his father. "Dad and I were going to draw up plans for the canoe trip, but I guess it can wait. I'd like to come, Mr. Brooks."

"Canoe trip?" Kip said.

"Yes," Dan said, "Dad and I have taken three. This year we're going for a week or two down the Trent Canal."

Canoe trip! But that would mean Dan would be gone for the rest of the summer! Suddenly he saw all the happy times, the swimming and paddling in the cove, the confidences on the shore, as over and done. But there was still the dog. Now he just had to get the dog. "Can we go now?" he said. "To see about the dog, I mean."

It did not take them long to reach the cottage. Len Big Canoe sat under the tree as if he had never moved, and the dog beside him. He growled as he saw them all approach but then wagged his tail and bounded out to meet them. Kip knelt down to pat him. "Good old Scout," he said. "Good old thing. Look, Dad, isn't he just about perfect?"

"He's a fine dog," Mr. Brooks said. "We'll go over and have a chat with Mr. Big Canoe about him."

The boys waited in the lane. Then Kip saw his father turn and come towards them. "You have a birthday coming up soon, it seems to me," he said. "August twenty-second?"

"Yes, Dad." Kip swallowed hard.

"Well, he's all yours as an early present. I've just bought him from Mr. Big Canoe."

Kip did not know what to say. He flung himself down and buried his face in the dog's coat. "Oh, Scout, you're mine! My very own dog! Do you hear that? Oh, boy! My own dog!"

"Take him over now to say good-bye to his master," Mr. Brooks said. "And watch him. He may not want to leave."

But the dog only whined when the old man put out his hand and touched him. Kip felt suddenly sorry for old Len. "I'll look after him really well, sir," he said. But the Indian could not hear. He nodded and smiled sadly as they went off towards the car.

The dog lay quite still all the way home. He followed Kip with a bound through the cedars to the cottage.

"Mom! Edna! Come and see, quick!" Kip shouted. Then he saw them on the beach and boy and dog leaped down together.

"Well, I never!" said Edna. "What have we got here, a star boarder?"

"He's mine, Edna! Dad got him for my birthday! Isn't he

the best-looking dog you've ever seen? Mom, don't you think so?"

Mrs. Brooks smiled. "Your father said he'd have to be pretty special before he'd get him, and I guess he is, all right. He was worth waiting for, wasn't he?"

"Gosh, yes! Come on, Scout! I'll race you to the cove and back again!" Kip felt like shouting at the top of his voice, as he ran and ran until he was out of breath and fell in a heap on the sand. The dog was all over him in a moment, licking his face and hands, calling him to play with short sharp yelps.

Later, at night in bed, he reviewed the events of the day. If only they had let Scout sleep beside him, he could have put out his hand and touched him, but his father had insisted on the verandah. When he awoke later, the house was in darkness and silence. He crept out past Edna's couch to where the dog lay on an old blanket. Scout raised his head and Kip could see his eyes shining. The tail thumped loudly on the floor. "Shh, boy!" Kip whispered. "They'll hear us." He stroked the dog's ears. "I just wanted to make sure you're still here. You're mine now, you know. You just wait, we're going to have more fun than anybody ever had!"

He heard Edna's bed creak and he slipped quickly back to his own room. He lay for a while thinking about Dan and how much he would miss him when he went away. He pictured Dan and his father camping together beside a deep still river, the firelight dancing on their faces. Nearby was a red canoe, the name Kanati flashing silver in the moonlight. Then he was asleep.

He was awakened in the morning by something cold and wet on his cheek. "Scout!" he shouted, and tumbled out of bed.

"No use having a dog unless he can say good morning to you," Edna called in. "He's been up with the lark!"

"Let's go for a swim together, shall we, Scout?" Kip sang out.

"Your father and mother have beaten you to it," Edna said. "They're in the water already."

It was that way every day until Saturday when Dan came. "Scout's wonderful in the water," Kip told him. "We've had him swimming races with us, and chasing sticks and everything!"

Mr. Brooks came to look for them on the beach. "Dan, Mrs. Brooks and I are going away for a short trip today," he said. "I hope you don't mind. It's something pretty important."

"I don't mind at all," Dan said. "We'll have fun."

Edna joined them on the sand in the morning with apples and a plate of cookies. She told Dan her ghost story. "It isn't much of a one," she said, "because it hasn't got an ending. Maybe you two could make up one for me."

Kip thought of the story when he was awakened that night. He had fallen into a deep sleep, after the hours in the water with Dan and the dog. There had been a noise outside, he knew that. Then he heard the sound of a car in the lane and heavy footsteps coming up the trail behind the cottage. He tried to stay awake but then the dog began to bark and he heard his father speak. If his father was still up, everything must be all right. In a moment he was sleeping soundly again.

Dan came on Sunday, just past noon, when they had all arrived home from the little country church near Bloomfield. They cooked hamburgers on the beach and Scout would have made off with the meat if Edna had not caught him trying to open the package.

"You two boys should go up to the clearing and look for more arrowheads," Mr. Brooks said. "Then it'll be nice and quiet around here, so I can take a little nap."

"Sure, we could do that," Kip said. "Coming, Dan?"

They fetched the spade and Kip dragged it behind him through the thick woods. A flock of red-winged blackbirds rose with startled cries from a nearby thicket.

"You'll never make an Indian hunter," Dan laughed. "I'll

have to teach you better woodcraft than that." Then he fell silent. They had broken through the woods into the small clearing.

Dan pointed. "Look!"

Floating without movement on the pond's surface was a red canoe, its paddles carefully placed across bow and stern. Kip dropped the spade and ran to the pond. "He got it!" he shouted. "I might have known he would! Isn't she a beaut?"

Dan followed slowly. He felt the smooth canvas. "Didn't you know your father was going to get it for you?"

"This isn't mine, silly!" Kip shouted. "It's yours. Look here." He pointed to the bow. There in shining silvery metal was the one word, *Kanati*.

Dan gaped. "But it couldn't be mine! Why would your father buy me a canoe?"

"It's a poor exchange for a life."

They wheeled, startled. Mr. Brooks stood at the edge of the clearing, smiling. "Did I do the right thing, Kip?" he said.

"Oh, Dad, it's super. But how did you get it here without me seeing it?"

"Your mother and I went to Peterborough to pick one out yesterday. They made a rush job on the name and delivered it very late . . ."

"Last night!" Kip interrupted. "So that's what all the noise was!"

"Pretty clever, aren't we?" Mr. Brooks winked at Dan. He could see that the boy was embarrassed. "I'm glad we're in time for the canoe trip, anyway, Dan."

Dan opened his mouth as if to speak and then fell silent.

"Boy!" Kip said. "When can we take it out?"

"It might be better to wait until supper now," Mr. Brooks said. "Edna said to tell you we're having fried chicken and if you don't turn up on time you'll only get the wishbone."

"What do we need that for?" Kip laughed. "We've got our wish already."

As Edna brought in the chicken, Dan turned to Mr. Brooks. "Sir," he said, "I have something to ask you."

"Go right ahead," Mr. Brooks said. "You know that we'll do anything for you we can, Dan."

"Dad and I have both been talking about it and we hope you'll say 'yes'."

"What is it?" Kip said.

"I've been on these trips lots of times before, ever since I was eight years old, and I know pretty well all there is to know about them," Dan went on hurriedly.

"Yes?" said Mr. Brooks.

"Well," Dan hesitated. "Dad wants me to take Kip on the canoe trip alone, and he'll stay home."

Kip almost choked on his food. He wanted to stand up and shout, "Let me go! This will never happen to me again! I just have to go!" But instead he sat there biting his lower lip and staring at his mother.

It seemed an eternity before she spoke. "Dan," she said, "I think this is something that Mr. Brooks and I will have to talk over together. Can we let you know in a day or two?"

Dan smiled, relieved. "Oh, yes. That will be all right."

Kip sat there stunned. He had fully expected that his mother's reply would be no. He wished that he could race round the table and hug her. Instead he attacked his supper as if his life depended on it.

Afterwards, Mr. Brooks helped the two boys to carry the wonderful canoe to the lake. Scout leaped in and out of it in a frenzy of barks so that they had difficulty in getting it off the beach. Dan took the bow and Kip the stern. It shot across the water like a slender red bird. With both parents and Edna watching from the shore, Kip knew that much could depend on his display of skill. He felt very sure of himself as the paddle dipped and lifted, dipped and lifted in the sunlit water.

"Do you think we could paddle up the lake to our cabin?"

Dan asked. "Dad and the family are there, and are they going to be surprised with this!"

"I'll ask. Can we paddle up to Dan's place?" he shouted. "It won't take us long!"

He could scarcely hear his mother's reply over the dog's excited barking. "Be careful!" she called. "And be back before dark."

As they headed the canoe into the northwest, Kip began to whistle for sheer joy. The sun was going down when they reached the cabin. The Stonefish family greeted the boys and the story of the canoe with surprised delight. By the time Dan and Kip set out for home the dusk was coming on, but a pale light still glimmered on the water. It was not hard for Kip to imagine himself already on a distant journey, searching for a camp-site with the night close at hand. Scout was waiting for them as they paddled in and he bounded into the water to meet them, almost upsetting the canoe.

Arrangements were made for Dan to paddle over with his father the next day to take the canoe to his cabin and then they drove him home. In bed later, Kip was determined not to sleep. He knew that the fate of his canoe trip was being decided at that very moment. The room felt close and he rose to push the window higher. He bumped against a chair with a loud thump. His door opened a crack and the light shone in.

"Are you awake, Kip?" It was his father.

"Yes, I just opened the window wider, that's all."

"Are you wide enough awake to come out and talk?"

Kip was out of the door in a second.

Edna made a wry face at him over her cup of tea. "We might have known you'd be awake in there," she said. "You'd better speak up in your own defence."

Kip felt half sick with excitement. "Can I go?" he said. "Please, Mom and Dad!"

"But you've never been away from home before, dear," his mother said.

"But I'm practically twelve now, and I'll be with Dan!"

"Yes," said Mrs. Brooks. "Dan has made quite a difference to a lot of things."

"You'll be outdoors all the time," his mother said, "and you're not used to it at all."

"I'd say he's been used to little else since we got here," Edna said without impertinence. "He's been living out in the sun, in the greenhouse and on the beach until he looks like an Indian himself."

"What about all the sleeping out?" Mrs. Brooks asked. "How would they know where to go?"

"They don't have to know much about that, Bet," Mr. Brooks smiled. "They just pull up at the most convenient place before the sun goes down. You don't look for motels on a canoe trip. You look for some pine branches and a good place to build a fire."

Kip's heart bounded at the thought of it. "Nothing would happen to me at night, Mom! Honestly it wouldn't!"

"You're sure you won't go looking for ghosts?" Edna grinned.

"Ghosts!" Kip snorted. "Who's scared of them?"

"Well, what do you think, Bet?" Mr. Brooks said. "Let's have your opinion. It's the most important."

There was genuine distress in Mrs. Brooks' voice. "Allan, I can't help being worried. What if there were an accident? I don't know if I care to spend a week or two in that kind of misery."

"Bet," Mr. Brooks said, "you know we have to let him try out his wings some time, don't you?"

"Some time!" Kip cried out. "But there just won't be any other time! I've got to go now! After all, Dan saved my life once and I'll never be silly like that again! Dan would see to that."

"I believe you," Mr. Brooks said. "Bet, I think he should go."

"Me, too," Edna said. "He couldn't be in better hands."

They all waited.

"All right," Kip's mother said, "I'll let him go."

Kip leaped up and the chair fell over with a crash. "Yippee!" he whooped. "I'm on my way!"

10. The Canoe Adventure Begins

"There's no reason why they can't start on Saturday since I'm not going along," Mr. Stonefish said. It was Tuesday afternoon, and he and Dan sat with Kip and Mr. Brooks at a round table discussion on the verandah.

"But they should have charts of the Trent Canal, shouldn't they?" Mr. Brooks asked. "I'd like to have some idea of the course myself."

"What are charts like, anyway?" asked Kip. Scout's head was on his knees and he was stroking the coarse coat.

"They show mileages and depths of water, Kip," Mr. Stonefish said, "and of course the position of all the locks you'll have to pass through."

"It's just like a picture of the whole trip, Kip," explained Dan, "with everything marked on it but the adventures we'll be having."

Mrs. Brooks hovered at the kitchen door. "And you will be careful with those adventures, won't you, Dan?"

136

"I promise, Mrs. Brooks," said Dan.

Kip's mother looked out at the clouds scudding across the sky. "I do hope the weather will improve before you start out," she sighed. "How will you ever pack enough warm clothing to keep you from getting a chill?"

Mr. Brooks laughed. "Bet, you can work up a good deal of heat paddling a canoe, even in a wind. As for the night, we'll see about a good strong tent."

Dan glanced at his father. "We weren't planning to take a tent, Mr. Brooks."

Mrs. Brooks looked shocked. "No tent!"

"A tent really slows down the journey, Mrs. Brooks," explained Mr. Stonefish. "There's always the problem of finding the right place to pitch it and the trouble of setting it up."

"They're really going to be roughing it then," Mr. Brooks said, "sleeping out under open sky."

"Not quite, Mr. Brooks," Dan said. "We sleep under the canoe."

"Using it as a kind of roof, you mean?" Mrs. Brooks asked.

"Right!" Mr. Stonefish drew a pencil and pad from his pocket. "Look here. We drive four stakes in the ground, if they're forked all the better. We rest the gunwales on them. The boys sleep lengthwise head to feet or feet to feet under this, with a ground sheet under them, and a couple of blankets to keep them warm."

Dan turned to Kip. "We have to have something over us to keep the dew off."

"All I can say is, I'm glad we brought along the young man's winter pyjamas," Edna called. "Maybe I should knit him a pair of bed slippers and a sleeping-cap."

Kip hooted with laughter. "Wouldn't I look dandy in those!"

"Who's to see you," Edna said, "but a couple of owls and a skunk or two?"

"A skunk!" Mrs. Brooks exclaimed.

Mr. Brooks smiled. "They're bound to meet a little wild life,

Bet. But you can rest assured there won't be any mountain lions or bears on the trail."

"They should have lots of company on the canal at this time of the year," Mr. Stonefish said.

"I suppose a good deal of American traffic uses the water-way," Mr. Brooks said.

"Oh, yes," Mr. Stonefish agreed. "They're a friendly lot, too, if you need any help."

"We'll remember that, Dan." Kip's eyes sparkled. "I just can't wait to get started." He glanced down at the dog. "There's only one thing. I just hate to leave Scout behind, that's all."

Edna poked her head round the door. "Don't worry, skipper. I'll treat that dog better than any dog has ever been treated before. He knows a good home when he sees it."

Mr. Stonefish rose. "I have to get back to the cottage I'm working on now, but we could get together tomorrow night if it's all right with you."

"Fine," said Mr. Brooks. "You and Dan come over for supper straight from work, and we can have a look at those charts and make a list of supplies."

"We'd better go shopping in Picton or Belleville the day after," Mrs. Brooks put in. "Kip needs a new warm jacket and heavier jeans, in case it stays cool."

The following night they began the list with ground sheets, blankets, a strong, thin-bladed belt knife and an axe.

There were dozens of smaller items to consider. "What about accidents?" Mrs. Brooks said anxiously. "What happens if they tear a hole in the canoe?"

"We'll mend it," Dan said. "We always take along a canoe repair kit, glue and canvas for patching, and a few brass tacks and nails."

"Add a canvas needle and twine to that, Dan," Mr. Stone-fish reminded him. "We have them both at home."

"And I shall be happy to add this ancient pot to the cook-ing department!" Edna held aloft a battered old saucepan.

"That's another thing," Mrs. Brooks said. "What will they take to eat?"

"They won't need to take too much, Bet," Mr. Brooks said. "There are villages all along the route where they can buy supplies."

"Anyway, we don't want fancy things to eat on a trip like that," Kip said.

"Oh ho!" Edna said. "I suppose you'd turn down a nice box of brownies if I make them for you to take along, eh?"

Kip grinned. "I mean fancy things to get ready, Edna. We'll sure take the brownies."

"There'll be lots of beans and bacon and things like that," Dan said, "and we'll eat our vegetables raw for the most part, and buy lots of fruit."

"Aren't we ever going to get to the charts?" Kip asked. "I want to see where we're going."

In a moment they had the first chart spread on the table. Even Mrs. Brooks and Edna had to have a peek. "Hmm," Edna sniffed. "Sure looks like an awful lot of water."

"They'll be covering about ninety miles altogether," Mr. Stonefish said. "It's one of the most beautiful waterways we know of for a trip like this. If the boys were older they could canoe the whole length of the system from Georgian Bay to Lake Ontario. It isn't made up of just one river as you can see. There are dozens of lakes and rivers flowing in from east, north and west to make up the waterway."

"Our own people used to travel up and down these rivers and streams a hundred years ago and more," Dan said. "There's another Reserve at Hiawatha on our trail. I have a friend there. We'll stop in and see him on the way."

"Champlain used this route, too," Mr. Stonefish said, "with the Huron Indians. For two hundred years after, it was a favourite trail of missionaries and fur traders."

"My goodness gracious!" Edna was leaning over the chart. "Look what I see here!"

"What is it?" Kip edged in beside her.

"Stirling! My old home town!" Edna pointed.

Dan leaned close. "There's a creek goes up to it from the canal."

"Rawdon Creek," Edna said. "It flowed right through the town." She smiled, remembering. "We used to skate on it all winter and swim in it all summer. Those were the good old days."

Mr. Brooks laughed. "You sound like a real old-timer, Edna. Come now, it wasn't all that long ago."

"Long enough," Edna sighed. "I'd kind of like to see the old place again some time, and some of the folks." She turned to Kip. "Why don't you drop up there and look the place over, and say hello to the ghost for me?"

"Sure I will!" Kip laughed, but the idea began to grow.

"What I'd like somebody to tell me," Mrs. Brooks put in, "is how we'll know which day to meet you in Trenton when you come back!"

"That shouldn't be too hard to find out," Mr. Brooks assured her. "We'll get the boys to give us a call at the store one night. I can wait around there until we hear. After all, there are villages with phones all along the way."

"Let's make it Thursday night for sure," Dan said. "We'll be well down the canal by then."

"Good," said Mr. Brooks, "and how about tomorrow morning for shopping in Picton?"

"We have quite a number of things at home," Mr. Stonefish said. "We hadn't really counted on buying much in the way of equipment. Dan and I usually manage on a shoestring."

"It'll be our shoestring you manage on this time," Mr. Brooks smiled. "You just provide the advice."

On Friday night Edna was still baking for the boys, this time a batch of muffins, when a knock came at the door. Kip ran to open it, the dog barking at his heels. He stepped back in surprise, his hand on Scout's collar. "Albert!" he exclaimed. "I didn't know you were coming!"

Edna dropped the muffin tin with a clatter. "Well, I never!" she said. "Look who's here!"

"Brought along an old friend of the boy's," Albert said. "Came to wish him luck. Heard he's setting out tomorrow."

"Mr. Mosely!" Kip gaped in astonishment.

Mr. Brooks rose from the fireside. "Come on in and sit down!" he called. "We're glad you came!"

"Look, Mr. Mosely and Albert, this is my new dog! His name's Scout!" Kip said. "Isn't he a beaut?"

"A good-looking dog," Mr. Mosely said briefly. "This might come in handy," he added, handing Kip a flat square parcel.

Kip knew he looked surprised, but he couldn't help it. Imagine gruff old Mr. Mosely bringing him a present! "Can I open it now?" Kip said.

"Only way you'll ever get to know what's inside!" Albert said. "Didn't come all this way to leave it in brown paper."

Kip tore at the heavy wrappings. He stared at the iron grill-work inside. "It's something to cook on, Edna. Look here!"

"What do you know!" Edna said. "Now I won't worry about you burning the beans and the bacon."

"Just be careful how you open it or you'll crack the joints," Mr. Mosely said. "I made it myself."

"Thanks a lot, Mr. Mosely," Kip said.

Albert had sidled over to inspect Edna's baking. "Smells pretty good, Edna," he said.

"I'll make some tea," Edna said, "and we'll have a celebration." Kip could not understand the embarrassed air about her. He felt a twinge of jealousy as he saw Albert reach out and pat her hand. He forgot it quickly as Albert turned and handed him a small package.

"What's this?" Kip asked.

"Not much," Albert said.

Mr. Brooks watched Kip undo the parcel. "An oilskin case! We'd forgotten about that!"

"What's it for?" Edna peeked over Albert's shoulder.

"To carry charts and matches in, Edna," Mr. Brooks said.

"It'll keep them dry in a rainstorm, and even if they get a tipping."

Kip saw the alarm on his mother's face. "Don't worry, Mom," he said. "Dan says I can swim like a fish." He turned to Albert. "Thanks, Albert, it sure was nice of you and Mr. Mosely to think of me."

When he awakened on Saturday morning he knew there was something special about the day. Then he remembered what it was. He leaped out of bed with a shout. "It's come!" He could hear voices outside in the lane. "Edna!" he called. "Who's here?"

"Just us chickens," Edna answered. "Your mother and dad are packing the car with all your stuff, and I'm getting ready to pack you with breakfast. Hurry up there! Your father wants to leave at eight."

Kip raced out to the dog. "Scout!" he shouted. "It's a wonderful day! The sun's shining!"

They were all in the car ready to leave when Kip said, "Can I say good-bye to Scout just once more, Dad?"

"Hurry it up, son," Mr. Brooks said. "Don't worry. He'll keep till you come home."

The dog was tied up in the shade of the cedar grove. "Oh, Scout," Kip said, "I wish like anything I could take you with me. I'll be back so soon you'll hardly know I've been away at all." The dog leaped up and licked his face. He whined softly. "He knows I'm going," Kip thought. He ran swiftly down the slope without looking back.

When they reached Lakefield where the trip was to begin, the charming little town with its wide stretches of parkland and water was already noisy with shoppers.

The Stonefish family was waiting for them, the red canoe tied to the dock, and the serious work of loading began. When the duffle was safely stowed, the ground sheets were drawn over it and the slender craft was ready for its maiden voyage.

"I'm starved," Dan said. "Can we eat now?"

"That's just where we're headed," his father said. "There's a big picnic table over in the park. Let's set up there."

Shortly before one Mr. Brooks led the way to the dock, an open bottle of ginger ale in his hand. "We can't break a bottle to christen her," he laughed. "Glass in the water would never do, so we'll pour it over." Even Nina and Tom cheered as he called, "I christen you Kanati!" Then he set the bottle down and shook hands with the boys. "Safe journey," he said seriously. "God keep you."

Kip was embarrassed at Edna's and his mother's affectionate hugs. He squirmed away as quickly as possible. But just before he stepped down into the canoe he gave his mother's hand a swift squeeze. "Don't worry, Mom," he said. "Everything's going to be wonderful!" Then he turned to Edna. "Tell Scout I'll be back soon and take good care of him for me."

"Sure thing, skipper!"

And then they were off, and the gay hues of summer on the dock were only a rainbow haze in the distance.

11. A Man in the Dark

"Hey, there, Champ! Not so fast! Do you want to get home before our folks do?"

Kip laughed and slowed his pace. It was true, he had been paddling for the first five minutes as if his life depended on it. They were rounding a bend in the river and approaching the bridge over which they had passed earlier in the car. Ahead lay their first lock, number twenty-six in the canal system. As they neared, they saw that the gates were closed. Another boat had passed through before them and the lockmaster was standing on the lock wall waiting for the channel to refill before he allowed them in. To their right a magnificent cruiser lay against the canal wall, waiting, like them, for entry. The words, ELDORA 11, ROCHESTER, were emblazoned in gold on her port side.

"Americans!" Dan said. "What a beauty of a boat!"

"Hi!" A round-faced young man with a crew-cut leaned over the stern and waved. "Where've you come from?"

"Home!" Dan called. "We're just beginning!"

The young man was joined by a small child. He whispered something to her and then shouted, "Good for you! You'll need lots of energy if you're doing it under your own steam!" The child tossed a large chocolate bar to them.

Dan caught it and Kip sang out, "Thank you!" Already things were beginning to happen!

"We'll look for you along the way," the man called. "Let us know if you'd like to hitch-hike!"

"I'm going up to help the lockmaster open the other gates," Dan said to Kip. "You keep the canoe steady. I'll be here to help you paddle out when the water's down."

Kip must cling to the rope dangling down into the water from the top of the canal wall, to keep the canoe steady while the water in the lock was lowered. This would permit the second set of gates to be opened so that they could pass out and down the river. The gates shut and the water began to flow out from under him with surprising speed. The canoe rocked and shuddered against the wall and his hands on the rope stung. Then the further gates were opened and Dan was again behind him, guiding the canoe in the wake of the big cruiser.

They moved away from Lakefield, passing along a buoyed channel, the river-bed and its rushing water in a deep wooded gorge on their left. The river widened when they rejoined it and the scene was one of placid beauty. Now and then the calm was broken by a motor-boat. It was all Kip could do to steady the canoe against the waves each one made.

"Don't worry, Kip," Dan said. "You'll get so used to this before we're finished, it'll be as easy as eating and drinking."

Later they passed a family trying to learn to water ski. Dan and Kip joined in the laughter from the shore as the father, a great husky man in a pair of scarlet bathing trunks, failed to keep his balance and plunged into the river. "Do you want to try?" he shouted to the boys.

"Not right now!" Dan replied. "We'll be back another day

when you've learned how and you can teach us."

The man came up dripping for the fifth time. "The way I'm going," he shouted, "you'd better make it in a year or two!"

Suddenly Kip lifted his paddle and the canoe rocked gently.

"Whoops!" Dan said. "What's up?"

"Bluebirds! A whole flock of them! They flew across the river and into the woods on the other side. I haven't seen a bluebird for years!"

"Our good luck charm," Dan grinned. "That means a happy journey."

Kip half turned in his kneeling position at the bow. "Do you mind if I stop for a minute?"

"Are you getting tired?" Dan asked. "We can put in if you want to."

"No, it's not that," Kip said. "I want to take my shirt off. I'm too hot."

"I wish you wouldn't," Dan said. "There's a light wind, and with that blazing sun you might sunburn."

Kip laughed. "Not me, Dan. I've got a fairly good tan already." He peeled off his shirt. The breeze felt wonderful on his back.

After three they put in to shore for milk and some of Edna's muffins. "You're tired, aren't you?" Dan said. "Do you feel like going on?"

"You bet I do!" Kip drank the milk eagerly. "I was thirsty, and that really tastes good!" He stretched himself out in the shade of a tall pine. "Gosh, Dan, it seems like we're miles and miles away from everybody already."

"I guess we are," said Dan. "That's what's good about this kind of trip. On a river you can really get away."

Kip leaped up. "Let's get going again! I feel super now."

Above Nassau the river widened and a great hill rose on their right. "It's a ski slide!" Kip shouted. "We should come back here in the winter!"

It was late afternoon when they reached Nassau Bridge

where the route carried them out of the Otonabee River and into the canal to their left. Three-quarters of an hour later they had come in sight of the hydraulic lift lock at Peterborough.

"There she is!" Dan said with a note of triumph. "The world's largest!"

Kip stared at the enormous structure. It was a gigantic affair, its weathered pillars soaring high in the air, the pontoons that carried the craft up and down, themselves like tremendous boats. Kip watched while one pontoon soared up towards them, and the other swung down, carrying a host of small craft. "Zowie!" he said. "You must have to know a thing or two to work that lock!"

"You do," Dan agreed. "The whole thing is worked by pressure. When one of the pontoons is up and opening into the upper stretch of the canal, the other is down opening into the lower stretch."

They entered the pontoon, and two small cruisers and a speedboat went with them. "It's like a water elevator," Kip remarked, enjoying the sensation and the splendid view. It stood behind them like a giant ship in dock as they pulled away.

"I think we'd better leave the city behind and get out into open country again before we find a camp-site," Dan said.

"It's okay with me," Kip said. He was feeling very tired with the hours of paddling but he would not have admitted it for the world.

It was half-past six when they beached the canoe on a small stretch of sand where a creek emptied into the river. There was a fine grove of cedars beyond smooth short-cropped grass. The hill behind them rose to a split rail fence.

"This is a good place to set the fire," Dan said. He gathered stones quickly while Kip searched for firewood among the trees. Dan noticed Kip's slow steps. "You're tired, Champ," he said. "Sit down here by the fire and I'll get everything ready."

Kip made no protest. He lay full length on the grass, every

limb aching. "I don't think I want anything to eat, Dan," he said. "I'm too tired."

"You just wait till it's all ready," Dan said. "You need some quick energy. Here, have a glass of milk while I get the beans and bacon going."

The aroma from the frying-pan was very tantalizing. When Kip put the first spoonful into his mouth he realized that he was ravenous. He ate so quickly that the food choked in his throat.

Dan saw him and laughed. "What did I tell you?"

"It's your cooking," Kip said. "It tastes super."

"You've earned that today," Dan said. "You're a real sport paddling so far the first day without moaning about it."

When the dishes were washed in the river and they sat in quiet content by the fire, Kip could hardly keep his eyes open. Dusk was just coming on when they settled down for the night under the canoe, the ground sheets and blankets in place. Kip lay listening to the frogs in the river. He peered out from under the makeshift shelter and saw the first stars shining in the luminous sky. Far off a dog was barking. He thought at once of Scout and felt suddenly lonely for the dog and the family at Kip's Cove. Then he fell into a deep sleep.

When he opened his eyes three hours later he could not imagine at first where he was. Darkness enveloped everything and his whole body was on fire. He groaned as he tried to sit up.

Dan was up in a second. "What's the matter, are you sick?" he said.

Kip bit his lip. "It's my back. I guess I did get too much sun after all."

Dan groped for the flashlight. "Turn over and I'll see how it looks." He gave a low whistle. "You've got a terrible burn. Keep still for a minute." He reached into a small bag and moved back to Kip, a tube in his hand.

"What's that?" Kip said. He could hardly bear to talk. It hurt so much.

"Some stuff for burns. Dad thought we might need it. Trust him, he thinks of everything."

Kip sighed with relief as the cold comforting salve was spread across his back. "Gosh," he said, "that feels good."

"What are you two doing here?"

At the sound of the harsh voice behind them Dan dropped the tube of ointment and Kip sat bolt upright. A flashlight shone in their faces, blinding them. Then they saw a man, thickset and ugly, standing at the edge of the cedar grove.

"You heard me. What are you doing here?" He came closer, staring at Dan.

"Just camping, that's all, sir," Dan said. "We didn't know this was private property."

"Well, it is. Get off and stay off."

Dan stared back at him. "You mean right now?"

"I mean right now." The man leaned against a tree and folded his arms. "And I'll stay here to see that you do."

"What shall we do?" Kip whispered. He was shaking but he would not let Dan see it.

"We'll have to move, Kip. I'm sorry."

"But how can we see to paddle in the dark?"

"We'll manage, don't worry. Come on, let's get all the stuff back into the canoe, quick."

The man continued to stare after them even when the canoe was launched.

"Take it easy," Dan said. "Don't worry. I can see where we're going if we keep in close to shore. You watch out for logs."

"I can see better now my eyes have got used to the dark," Kip said.

"How's your back?"

Kip laughed. "Gee, I was so excited about the man, I forgot all about it. It feels better with that stuff on it, anyway."

"There must have been a cottage back there behind the hill," Dan said. "Wouldn't you know we'd pick that spot with a whole river full of emptiness?"

They went very slowly, the night silence broken only by the rise and fall of the paddles and the sudden scurryings of small animals at the river bank. The sky was ablaze with stars.

"Let's try in here," Dan said after half a mile. "There's no hill here and I don't see a sign of a house anywhere."

The land was quite flat with a line of willows marking the entry of a small creek. They went up the creek very slowly and beached the canoe on the flats and tied it to a willow tree. The grass was longer here and it took them some time to bring all the supplies ashore and to set the canoe up on the stakes.

"I never thought I'd be able to say it with this sunburn," Kip said, "but I'm cold."

"I'll build a fire and we'll have some cocoa," Dan said. They sat in the firelight sipping the hot drink in silence.

"Why did he do that?" Kip said at last. "We weren't doing anybody any harm."

"It was probably me," Dan said.

"You?" Kip asked. "Why you?"

"Anybody can see I'm an Indian."

"What difference does that make?" Kip said.

"Oh, I don't know." Dan fingered his mug. "People often look down on Indians as a poor ignorant lot. We live on reserves by ourselves. We don't pay taxes, and it isn't until lately that they've thought of giving us the vote. Some people even think we don't go to school. They even expect us to do a war dance as we pass by."

"What if he did think all those stupid things," Kip said. "He still had no right to chase us off in the middle of the night."

Dan shrugged his shoulders. "He might have thought we were going to steal something. In some people's minds that goes with being poor and ignorant and not quite as good as somebody with a white skin."

Kip did not know what to say. It astonished him that anyone could look upon Dan as either poor or ignorant. To Kip he was rich in character and independence, and wise beyond words. There was nothing he wanted quite so much as to be like him.

"Don't worry about it," Dan said. "It doesn't worry me." He banked the fire. "If we don't turn in now we'll never want to get up in the morning."

Kip lay on his stomach and watched the comforting glow of the coals. Willows, ragged tree stumps and tall grasses made strange shapes in the darkness. Watching them, he fell quickly asleep.

The rattling of spoon against saucepan wakened him in the morning. Dan was already at the fire making breakfast.

"Porridge!" Kip said. "Edna could never get me to eat that at home."

"You'll like it here," Dan grinned. "You need something that sticks to your ribs, as the old-timers say. How'd you sleep?"

"Wonderful!" Kip sat up.

"How's the sunburn?"

"It feels a lot better this morning," Kip said. "That stuff you put on was really good."

"Keep your shirt on today, don't forget," Dan warned. "It's going to be hot but you'll have to put up with it for a while."

The air was hot even when they set out, and the sky clear. "We'll stop off for a swim soon," Dan promised. "That will keep you cool."

They had been paddling for over a mile when Dan called a halt and put in to a nearby bank. "I want to see how far to the next lock," he said. "I forgot to check the chart this morning." He opened the oilskin package. "About five miles," he figured. "This should be a good easy stretch, so relax and don't try to hurry if your back is still sore."

But Dan had forgotten it was Sunday. All along the way wherever summer settlements crowded the shore, pleasure craft slowed their passage. But the going was pleasant. The farm landscapes they passed were golden with wheat ripening in the August sun, and deep green with groves of cedars.

"There's another creek along here somewhere," Dan said. "That should be a good place to land the canoe."

When they came to it, and plunged off the little point into the water, the cold stung Kip's back. But the pain was soon gone. "Keep in the shade!" Dan warned. "If you get any more sun on that back, that'll be the end of the trip for us."

After the swim the heat in mid-river was intense. They went on in silence until two hours later they had reached Wallace Point. "Anything you want in the store?" Dan said to Kip.

"You bet!" Kip sang out. "An ice-cream cone! I'm just about roasted!"

They sat licking their cones, dangling their legs over the canal wall. The water was noisy with week-end boats, and several families were enjoying a late breakfast in the picnic ground. The boys were glad to leave the heat of the shore and strike out for mid-river, and when the heat became too oppressive there, they ducked into the shelter of overhanging trees and hugged the shore-line.

"Can you get very far up any of these creeks?" Kip asked as they passed a small stream that disappeared into a thicket of willows.

"Sure, up some of them," Dan said. "Why?"

"Oh, no reason. I just wondered."

"You weren't thinking of going up Rawdon Creek to Stirling, were you?" Dan asked.

Kip turned, astonished. "How did you know that's what I was thinking?"

Dan laughed. "Because that's what I've been thinking myself! I don't see why we couldn't have a try at it anyway. It would be fun to tell Edna we'd been. Who knows, we might even find her ghost for her!"

"Do you really think so?" Kip gave a little shiver. "It sure would be fun."

"Let's do it then." Dan scooped up a handful of water and splashed it on his hot face. "That feels better. Try it yourself."

"How far to Rawdon Creek?" Kip asked, enjoying the water dribbling inside his shirt.

"Oh, a long way yet," Dan said. "That'll come near the end of the trip. We'll figure out how we'll do it when we get there."

It was high noon when they arrived at Bensfort Bridge. Even the small restaurant seemed cool after the merciless heat of the sun on the river. "We'll be softies and buy our meal today," Dan said. "Somehow I couldn't face a fire right now."

After lunch they bought more supplies for later on in the day. "It'll be cooler then," Dan said. "We'll find the shadiest spot we can to camp in, and make a big meal tonight close to sundown." Then they were on their way again.

The river turned south in a wide sweeping arc at Campbelltown. "Campbelltown was once called Onigon," Dan told Kip as they followed the bend in the river. "It's an Indian word meaning the pulling up of stakes."

"That's a funny name to call a place," Kip said. "Was there a reason?"

"You bet. At one time the Mississauga Indians chased our people the Mohawks down the river. The Mohawks camped here, hoping to make a stand, but when they knew the Mississaugas were close they pulled up stakes and made off down the river. So there you have the name."

As they followed the southerly flow of the water, the high thin clouds in the sky began to thicken and the heat became less intense. A haze began to filter across the sun. "That feels better on the sunburn," sighed Kip. "I was hoping for sun on the whole trip, but I'm kind of glad to say good-bye to it for a while."

"We may be paddling in rain before we're through," Dan said. "But maybe a cloudy day or two would fix up your burn for good. Then we could spend more time swimming."

"Do you think it would hurt the burn to go in once more today?" Kip asked.

"I don't think so. We'll be at the Hiawatha Reserve in less

than an hour and maybe Tom will come in with us."

Kip guessed that Tom was the friend of whom Dan had spoken and he looked forward eagerly to meeting him. It was half-past two when they passed the wide mouth of Kent Creek and came in sight of the Reserve. They paddled among the rushes to moor their canoe to a huge willow.

"You'll need to take off your shoes here and wade in," Dan advised. "It's pretty swampy."

The water felt wonderful on his feet and legs. Kip hoped that they could get the formalities over quickly so that they could swim. "Tom's house is up here in the trees," Dan said. "He has a part-time job at the store so he may not be home."

The boy was hammering at the front stairs of the small cottage mending a step. He rose to greet Dan with a wide grin. A look of uncertainty appeared on his face when he caught sight of Kip. He whispered something quickly to Dan. Dan smiled. "He wants to know if your dad hired me as a guide for you."

Kip laughed. "He's my guide without being hired. He taught me how to do the crawl and how to paddle a canoe."

"If Dan's teaching you, you'll do okay," Tom said. "Where are you guys going?"

Dan explained the whole trip briefly. "I sure wish I could come with you," Tom said, "but I couldn't leave my job."

"Well, at least you can come in swimming with us," Kip said. "And boy! Am I looking forward to that! I'm baked on both sides!"

The water beyond the reeds was deliciously cool.

"Where are you headed for the night?" Tom asked later as they sat under the willows, "Spook Island?"

"Spook Island!" Kip said. "Zowie! There's a name for a place!"

"It's only a name though," Dan said. "I haven't ever heard of anybody finding spooks there yet."

"Sure, but there's always a first time," Tom said with a grin.

"I wish I was going to be there and I'd dream up a few tricks to scare you!"

"Oh, you would!" Kip laughed. "Where is this Spook Island, anyway?"

"In Rice Lake," Dan told him. He searched for the oilskin package in the duffle and produced a chart. "Look here, we'll be leaving the Otonabee in about half an hour and coming out on the north shore of the lake."

"There's Spook Island," Kip said. "Almost opposite the mouth of the river!"

"That's it," said Dan. "Are you game to camp there for the night?"

"Sure," Kip said. "Why not?"

Tom watched them go with longing plainly written on his face. "Does he have to keep the job?" Kip asked.

"Tom's father left home three years ago," Dan said, "and nobody knows where he is. His mother takes in washing from the summer people and Tom has to work all his spare time from school to help out."

Kip turned to wave his paddle. He remembered his own job with Mr. Mosely, done purely for his own pleasure, and how lucky he was that it had brought him such adventure. And meanwhile, before him, lay the night on Spook Island.

12. Midnight on Spook Island

It was just past four when they headed out past the black and red buoys that marked the entrance to Rice Lake, and on towards the small island in the distance. It was heavily wooded and they had no difficulty choosing a camp-site. They drew the canoe far up on the land because, as Dan said, there was a storm brewing somewhere, and Rice Lake waters were known for their treachery in bad weather. They had just finished unpacking when they heard the whistling. It seemed to come from a bend in the shore-line to their left where the water formed a little cove.

"We've got company," Dan said. "Let's go and see who it is."

They found the man sitting astride a rock, his fishing-line cast far out in the deep water. He was small and wiry, his face wrinkled with weather. The hair that stuck out in wisps from his dirty cap was matted and gray. "Why don't you git a line in here," he said, "and fish for your supper?"

"Good idea," Dan agreed. "I'm starved. Fresh fish would go down really good. We'll get our tackle."

The old man showed them the best place to cast. "You have a go at it, Champ," Dan said. "I get lots of chances to fish."

Dan explained some of the tricks of casting. After Kip's second try the sinker landed far out in the tiny cove where the water was moving scarcely at all. "That's the place," the stranger said. "You'll catch a big one there. Ever hear tell of the big one they caught up Chemong way?"

"No, I haven't," Dan said. "Have you, Kip?"

"I don't even know where Chemong way is," Kip admitted.

"It's a lake in the Kawartha region," Dan said. "It's on one of our charts, but not on the part we're using."

"What about the fish?" Kip asked.

The old man took a plug of chewing tobacco from his sagging pocket and bit off a generous helping. He held it towards the boys. "Don't suppose you want to try this?"

"No! No, thank you!" Dan said hastily.

"Seems like there's an island up in this here Lake Chemong called Steamboat Island," the man began. "Seen it myself, so I know. It used to be a real big one, too, but most of it disappeared overnight without anybody findin' out why." The old man pulled gently on his rod as the current tugged at it. "Anyway, seems as if one old Indian knew why and he told the rich fellows he was guidin' for one day while they was out fishin'. They was boastin' about all the big ones they caught and he says he caught the biggest fish in the country. They ask him to tell where and how, and he tells 'em. Seems that Indian was fishin' one day off this here Steamboat Island and he caught one great big muskie. It was that big that it dragged the Indian's boat behind it until he was so fearful he jumped ashore, took a turn round the island to fasten his boat-line and left to fetch help in Bobcaygeon. Whatdya suppose happened?" The old man stopped his chewing dramatically.

"What?" the boys chorused.

"When he came back, that there fish had made off, dragging the island with him. That's why it's never been the same since."

Kip and Dan hooted with laughter. "I'll have to remember that one to tell Dad," Dan said.

The fisherman peered at them from half-closed eyes. "I got lots more stories if you'd like to hear 'em. I suppose you know the one about this place."

Dan drew in the line Kip held and helped him to cast again. "Spook Island? No, that's something we'd really like to know."

"It's a true story, this one. It goes back to Indian days."

"More Indians!" Kip said.

"Place was full of 'em round here once," the stranger said. "Just full of 'em." He glanced quickly at Dan. "What tribe you belong to?"

"The Mohawks at Tyendinaga."

"Funny thing," the older man said, "there was Mohawks mixed up in this affair. Leastwise there was Iroquois and that's what the Mohawks belonged to."

"Were they on this island?" Dan asked.

"They come here after the Ojibways had hid their women and children on this island for safekeepin' in the wars. The Iroquois attacked and killed 'em all." The man gazed at Dan speculatively. "Your people in those days was killers."

Kip sprang to Dan's defence. "Most Indians were," he said almost in anger. "That's the way they had to live."

The old man patted Kip's arm with a dirty hand. "Don't get riled now. I know all that. In those days they didn't know no better. Now the fellas that run the world is supposed to know better and all they've done is figure out bigger and better ways than tomahawks to kill off thousands of people."

"Dad said to me once that the Indians in the old days had some good things about them, too," Dan said. "And it wasn't our fault they were savages, any more than it would be Kip's fault here, if his great-great-great-grandfather had been hanged for sheep stealing!"

"That's a pretty good way of puttin' it," the man said, giving Dan a toothless grin. "It's what you do with your own livin' that adds up, not what your folks did before you."

"And what do you do?" Kip asked suddenly. "For a living, I mean?"

"Just fishin' mostly, and knockin' about." He nudged Kip's arm. "Take a look at your line. You got somethin'."

"I have! I have!" Kip whooped. "Dan, help me!"

Together they landed the catch, a large bass. "Boy! I can't wait to get that on the grill!" Dan smacked his lips. "Come on, Champ! Let's go!"

"You never let me finish the tale I was tellin'," the old man said. "Don't you want to hear it?"

"Sure,' said Kip. "What is it?"

"They tell me there's haunts on this island from the Indian days, haunts from the killin' I was tellin' you about."

"Haunts?" Kip said.

Dan laughed. "He means ghosts. Don't you believe a word of it. It's just a story."

"Don't be too sure, fella." The man put the three fish he had caught in a large tin. "I talked to folks who's heared 'em."

"Who is 'them'?" Kip asked, his heart beating a little faster.

"The ghosts of the women and children who was killed by the Iroquois." The old man peered knowingly at Dan. "If anybody'd hear 'em and see 'em, it'd be you two, eh?" With that he shouldered his untidy fishing tackle, climbed the rocks and wandered off into the bushes.

Kip stared after him in silence. Dan poked him playfully in the ribs. "Come on now, pal, you're not falling for that story, are you? Forget it, and let's go eat!"

Later, with the fish sizzling over the fire, Kip found it easy to laugh over the story. Their camp-site was so protected by a wall of pines, and so elevated from the sound of the water, that it seemed to hold for him almost the security of a house. They enjoyed every mouthful of fish.

"Boy!" Kip leaned against a moss-covered log. "I could burst!"

"Me, too!" Dan said. "I'm glad we don't have to paddle anywhere after that."

"How big is this lake, anyway?" Kip asked.

"Pretty big. About thirty miles long and five miles wide. It got its name from the wild rice growing around the shores. Our people used to gather it, and some still do, I guess. But a lot of it got diseased and there isn't half as much as there used to be."

"What's that Kawartha district you were talking about to the old man?"

"It's a chain of fifteen lakes, from Rice to Balsam," Dan said. "Of course there are plenty of rivers mixed up in it, too. Kawartha is an Indian word meaning bright water and happy lands."

Kip smiled to himself. That described to perfection the country through which they had passed in the last two days.

"I guess the Indians in those days didn't have time to see how nice everything looked," he said lazily. "They'd be too busy hunting up things to eat."

"Oh, they didn't have too much to worry about," Dan said, "not with forests full of game and fish."

"What kind of animals did they eat?" Kip asked. "Deer and bear?"

"Yes, and elk, beaver and even porcupine. Wild fowl were favourites, turkey, geese and ducks."

"Huh," Kip said. "They didn't eat so differently from what we eat now."

"No, they had wild fruits, too. Plums, raspberries, strawberries and blueberries. They ate lots of nuts, of course, and squeezed the oil from them, and from sunflower seeds, to make Indian butter."

"Did they eat bread?" Kip said.

"Sure, they made it from Indian corn." He reached into a nearby bag. "How would you like to pop some before we settle down for the night?"

"Some corn?" Kip eyed the yellow package in surprise. "Where did you get it?"

"At the store today. We can do it in the fry pan."

They took turns shaking the pan over the hot embers and had to cover it with a tin plate when the corn shot out in all directions. They found the butter and salt and applied liberal amounts of both. Kip sighed when the bowl was empty. "Gosh," he said, "I'm stuffed."

Dan looked up at the darkening sky. "The clouds are getting heavier. I guess we'll have some rain before tomorrow's done. It seems to have got awfully close again."

Kip slapped his arm. "Yes, and the mosquitoes know it, too."

"It looks as if we might get a few around here," Dan said. "I'll set a little smudge and keep it going for a while. That should drive them away."

Kip watched while Dan found some green leaves and laid them on the coals. The ensuing cloud of smoke made the air a little heavy but at least the mosquitoes were discouraged.

The boys set about making their bed. "We're lucky we've got good pine boughs in this spot," Dan said, bringing two large ones to put under the ground sheets. "We won't need blankets tonight. It's too warm."

The night was so still that Kip could hear the clear joyous notes of a white-throated sparrow in the woods. Small things rustled as they scurried through the underbrush, and the water whispered like silk against the shore. Far off, against the southern shore, he could see lights flickering, and then he heard voices singing. He sat up.

"What's that, Dan?" he said. "I hear singing."

"Somebody having a beach party," Dan said. "Those lights are Gore's Landing. There's a big government wharf there,

and a lot of boating and fishing. I'll take you there one day."
He turned on his side. "Better get off to sleep now. We should
get an early start in the morning."

"Okay." Kip lay listening to the voices, rising and falling
across the water, and then he was asleep.

When he awakened he did not move. The sound that had
disturbed him came again, a long low moaning from the
woods to the north. The skin on his back and up into his hair
prickled. He sat up slowly, listening. It came once more, passing this time towards the south. He remembered the old man's
'haunts' at once, and for one brief moment considered diving
under the blanket and staying there. He forced himself to
stand up and grope for a flashlight.

"What in thunder is that?" Dan had leaped to his feet.

"I was just going to find out," Kip said.

"Not without me, pal. Wait till I get my jeans on." Dan
stood still as the noise came again. "Gosh, that's an odd one,
that is."

"It couldn't be a wolf, could it?" Kip asked. He wished his
legs would stop shaking.

"I doubt it," Dan said. "Do you want to stay here while I
go and have a look?"

"Golly, no!" Kip said. "I'm coming, too!"

In a moment they were feeling their way through the bush,
the flashlight picking out the path. The moaning had stopped.
When it broke out again it was to their right. They turned,
stumbling over tangled undergrowth and frightening the small
animal life.

"This looks like a wild goose chase," Dan said, obviously
puzzled.

Kip was cheered that all seemed normal. "You mean a wild
ghost chase!"

Dan's laughter sounded very loud in the night. "That's a
good one," he said. "Anyway, ghost or not, let's go back to
camp and forget it. We may find out what it was in the morning."

As they stumbled wearily into the camp-site Dan stopped short and flashed his light over the scene. "Jumping Jeepers!" he gasped. "What a silly fool I've been!"

"Why?" Kip said.

"Just take a look!" Dan panned the light slowly over the ground. Everything was in wildest disorder.

Kip stood with his mouth open. "What happened?" he whispered. "Was it an animal?"

Dan groaned and sank to a log, his head in his hands. "Why didn't I use my common sense?"

"What do you mean?" Kip said. "It wasn't your fault."

"Oh yes it was." Dan shook his head ruefully. "Our friend the old man has been visiting us."

"The old man!" Kip was astonished. "You mean the one who was fishing with us?"

"That's him," Dan said. "He was your ghost, you can be sure of that."

"You mean he made that noise to scare us?"

"You bet he did. To draw us away from camp so he could help himself, and we were silly enough to fall for it."

"But that's just plain stealing!" Kip protested.

Dan nodded. "Uh huh, that's right. You'd better find him and tell him that."

"But what can we do?" Kip said.

"Not a thing. He probably knows this island like a book, and I'd like to bet he's half-way across to the mainland now in a row-boat." Dan examined the supplies. "Oh, well, it's not as bad as it could be. We still have bacon left for breakfast and matches to light a fire."

"Why would anybody be so mean?" Kip said. "Trying to scare us and then stealing our stuff?"

Dan shrugged his shoulders. "You know what they say: it takes all kinds to make a world." He put the bed straight. "Let's settle down. We'll take stock of our supplies in the morning. I cut enough firewood last night for breakfast, so we won't miss the axe yet."

"Good night!" Kip sang out. "See you at the crack of dawn!" Excitement kept him awake for a while, and just when sleep was taking hold there was another sound, no wailing this time but a soft thud followed by a rattle.

"Dan!" Kip poked him with his foot. "Wake up!"

"Mmm?" Dan yawned sleepily. "What's up now?"

Kip leaned close. "I think he's come again. I heard a noise!"

Dan stared into the darkness. Suddenly a pair of eyes lit up the night beyond the fire. "Hold it!" he whispered. "I think it's a skunk after the tins! Don't move or we'll have had it!"

They lay, scarcely breathing, while the animal nosed about. In a few moments he ambled off into the bush. Dan waited until the white flag of a tail had disappeared and then he sat up. He began to laugh. "Gosh, Champ," he said, "there's one thing for sure. You're not going to forget this night in a long, long time!"

13. Birthday in a Barn

"Now if I can only find a can of beans we'll be all right."

Kip's eyes opened at the sound of Dan's voice. The air was filled with the fragrance of wood-smoke and sizzling bacon. He grinned at Dan. "Hi!" he said.

"Hi, Champ!" Dan found the beans and opened the tin. "I thought I'd let you sleep in this morning after last night. Our friend took the eggs. I hope he's enjoying them this morning."

Kip yawned. "Oh, well, I like beans." He wondered what Edna would say if she heard him say that. A week ago she could not persuade him to look at one. He thought of Scout and hoped that Edna was taking him for a run along the beach.

"How about a swim while these things are heating?" Dan asked. "Do you think the burn will stand it?"

Kip flexed his back. "It's almost all gone. I'd love a swim." They plunged off the rock together. The lake was very still and the distant shore-line muffled in a blanket of haze. The lowering clouds formed dips and swirls as if painted with a broad wet brush. Around them the whole world was wrapped in grey.

Dan came up with the water streaming from his brown face. "We'll have to get going, I guess. I don't like the look of that sky. The sooner we get away from the island the better."

"Will it rain this morning?" Kip clambered up on the slippery rock, shivering.

"It's hard to tell. From the way things look, there's probably cool air moving in and that means a high wind," Dan said. "We won't worry about it. We'll just take things as they come."

Within half an hour, the camp-site tidied and the fire well doused with water, they were in the canoe moving off towards Tick Island to the east. They reached it half an hour later and struck in to the mainland along a strange outcropping of grasses pointing, on the surface of the water, in a straight line to the north shore.

Kip stared at it. "What's this, Dan?"

"The ruins of an old railway trestle under the water," Dan told him. "It used to run from Cobourg to Peterborough."

"We'll have to be kind of careful here," Kip said.

"You just keep paddling," Dan said. "I'll keep us on the right track."

"How do you tell if there's anything under the water that might hit the canoe?" Kip asked.

"Usually by what's happening on top of the water," Dan replied. "You'll see V marks or swirls on the surface if it's a log, or water heaving up if it's a round stone. If it's a lot of sharp stones, the water boils."

They came in to shore at the spot on their chart marked Picnic Point and saw through the overhanging willows, the cottages of Hiawatha village.

"We'll keep as close to the shore as possible," Dan said. "With some weather on the way, this lake could get pretty rough in a matter of minutes."

Some while later they navigated the channel between Harris Island and the mainland and came out into a bay. Dan pointed. "There's something doing up there," he said.

Kip followed his finger. High on a rolling green hill he could see people moving against the sky like figures in a silhouette show. "What is it, anyway?" he asked.

"I don't know, but we're going to find out." Dan found a hideaway for the canoe among some reeds. "It'll be quite safe here," he assured Kip. "Let's go."

The air was close away from the water and their faces were flushed as they reached the summit. Smooth grass-covered mounds twisted beside one another across the hill-top. Half a dozen young men and women were bent over, grubbing in the brown earth. Beyond the tents at the edge of the path stood two glass-fronted showcases. "Let's have a look at this," Dan said.

Kip stared at the arrowheads and broken pieces of pottery. "Boy!" he said. "They must be finding stuff here!"

"Let's go and speak to the man over by the tents," Dan said. "He must know something. He's in uniform."

The man saw them as they came up under the huge trees. "Good morning!" he called. "You're our first visitors of the day."

"Good morning," Dan said. "What's this all about, anyway?"

"This is the Serpent Mounds Park," the guide said. "These people are digging for Indian relics."

"Just like us at home," Kip said. "We found an arrowhead beside our creek. But what does Serpent Mounds mean?"

"You see the way the grass-covered humps snake across the hill like a serpent?" the man asked. "These were burial grounds used by the Indians some eighteen hundred years ago. We're now searching for relics here to find out how they lived."

"Zowie!" Kip said. "I'd like a job like that. Wouldn't you, Dan?"

"Sure," Dan said.

The man smiled. "You have to be sixteen before you can work here. Wait until you're in high school. Then you can come and join us."

Kip eyed the wooden pegs marching in orderly rows to mark the squares of excavation. "Don't you think we could dig just for a minute right now?"

"Perhaps," the guide said. "We could get one of the students to keep an eye on you." He leaned across the rope and spoke to one of the diggers.

The latter straightened up and smiled. "Hi! Come on down!" He put a small trowel in Kip's hand. "Use this with care and slowly. Every inch of the earth has to be gone over, but if you're rough you may destroy something before you get it out of the ground."

"I'll be careful." Kip prodded the soil gently. He was disappointed when, after five minutes, he had found nothing.

The young man clapped him on the back. "Don't look so glum, pal. Sometimes we're here for days and we don't find a thing. It's the hope that keeps us going."

The air had grown more humid when, after lunch, they were ready to go again. It made paddling an effort, but Dan insisted that they make good time. "If there's a storm coming, let's get off the lake and into the Trent River," he said. He brought out the chart and showed it to Kip. "Look here. This is the distance we have to travel. If we can be well past Cameron Point when the rain begins, I'll be happier."

Kip paddled with all his might. After two hours his body was drenched with perspiration and his face scarlet. He sighed with relief when he heard Dan's voice, "Relax now! Take it easy. We're coming into the Trent."

They were passing the wide swampy mouth of the Ourse River and the channel had narrowed. Because of the swampland and the danger of submerged piers they were forced to keep to the middle of the river. "Why don't we put in somewhere here?" Kip asked. "We don't have to keep on going, do we?"

"I'm looking for a place Dad and I found on our last trip," Dan said. "But I think it was closer to Hastings."

The first crack of thunder broke over their heads with such fury that they both stopped paddling and gaped up into the sky. "Head for the shore fast!" Dan shouted.

A sudden high wind drove the canoe against the shore and they had difficulty mooring it. Their clothes were soaked in an instant. "We'll keep the ground sheets on the duffle!" Dan shouted, the water pouring down his face. "We can always dry ourselves off but it wouldn't be so easy with the bedding and the food."

"Do you think it will last long?" The rain on Kip's tired body was wonderfully refreshing.

"It's my guess that it's an all-night affair," Dan said. "We may have to put up somewhere to sleep."

"Do you want me to go and look for a place?" Kip offered.

"Gee, would you?" Dan caught at the canoe's mooring rope. "While you're gone, I'll try to drag this thing round into this creek. It'll be safer there and more sheltered."

Kip scrambled through the bushes, the branches lashing his face. He came out into a farm pasture where a herd of cows were hunched together under an old elm. Through the rain he saw a large new barn with a steel roof directly ahead of him. Beyond it was an old stone house with bright red shutters. An enormous clap of thunder sounded so close that he plunged forward and took shelter under the eave of the barn. Beside him was a doorway, the bottom closed, the upper half open. He could hear a loud clear whistle.

"Say, you're wet!" The voice came out of the darkness inside. "Come on in." The speaker was a tall, lanky young man with red hair and a friendly grin. "Did you come down with the rain?"

"I sure look like it, don't I?" said Kip. "We just came in off the lake in a canoe."

"Hey, Sam!" the man called. "Come and see what we've got here!"

Another man appeared out of the gloom of the barn, older but also red-haired. "Hello, what can we do for you?"

The younger man spoke before Kip could answer. "Sam, I think he heard we needed somebody to clean out those stalls and fork manure down in the sheep run." He winked at Kip. "How about it, son?"

"Sure, I'd love to help, if only I had some dry clothes," Kip said. "I've always wanted to live on a farm."

The older man laughed. "Bill's only pulling your leg, boy. What's your name?"

"Christopher Brooks. My friend Dan is down at the river mooring the canoe. We're on a trip and the storm drove us in."

"Pretty wet night for camping."

Kip jumped at the sound of the third voice behind him. Its owner was shorter than the other two but there was a marked likeness to them.

The one called Bill saw Kip's surprise. "Oh, there's one more to come yet," he said, "but he's in town getting a new blade for the mower. I'm Bill, and this is Sam," he pointed to the older man and then to the shorter, "and this is Milt. Joe'll be back before supper."

"All brothers?" Kip asked.

"That's right," Sam nodded. "I see your friend on his way up. He's a little damp, too."

There was a round of introductions as Dan came in. "I brought some dry stuff up in the ground sheet," Dan said. "Would you mind if we changed into it somewhere?"

"I'd say you'd better," Milt grinned. "Bill, you take these two up to the house and make them at home."

"We're four bachelors," Bill said, as they entered the kitchen. "Don't look too hard!"

"Gosh," Dan said. "Do you do all your own housework and cooking?"

Bill threw them each a large towel. "You bet we don't," he laughed. "Sister Mary lives out there across the potato patch.

She comes and does it for us." He led them upstairs to a neat bedroom. "She's the eldest and she's run us all our lives and now she hates to give it up!"

Kip glanced about him. "You know," he said, "I was kind of hoping we could sleep in the barn."

"You can, too, if that's what you want," Bill said. "There's a loft full of hay out there."

"We can bring our own blankets up," Dan said.

"It's settled then," Bill said. "Come on down to the barn now and we'll do a few more chores before Mary comes over to cook supper."

The rain sounded warm and friendly on the barn roof as the boys helped the brothers.

"How old are you two?" Sam asked.

Kip wondered at Dan's startled expression. "I'm eleven and Dan's fourteen," he said.

Then Mary arrived at the house, a tall slender woman with dark hair looped in an old-fashioned bun. They sat down at the table soon, Mary waiting on them from the kitchen.

"What's that you've got in the box, Mugs?" Bill asked. "One of your specialties?"

"Just a chocolate cake," she said, "and if you behave yourself you might get some."

Joe arrived while they were sampling the cake, a big jolly man with a smooth red face and twinkling blue eyes.

"Come on, Joe," Bill called. "We've got two river pilots for supper tonight."

When Mary had gone the men asked the boys about their homes and their journey. Kip felt a sudden pang of homesickness as they talked about Scout and Kip's Cove. They seemed very far away.

"Lucky kids to take a trip like that," Bill said. "That's something I've always wanted to do myself but there was always hay to cut or pigs to feed or cows to milk."

"You're lucky to be able to do all that," Kip said.

"Well now, we're not going to hold you back," Milt said. "Come on out to the barn after supper and you can do all the chores."

Kip grinned. "Even milk a cow?"

"We've got an electric milker," Bill said, "but I think we could arrange one cow for you."

The milking was a complete failure but caused a great deal of laughter. Kip and Dan forked down hay from the loft for the cattle and fed the calves from a battered pail. Later, in rubber boots much too large for them, they waded down to the creek with Bill to bring up the bedding. Their blankets were soon spread on the hay and they were ready for sleep. "You've got your flashlight," Bill said. "I couldn't leave the lantern, anyway. It's too dangerous."

They sank back on the hay as the lantern disappeared and darkness closed around them. Light filtered in through the cracks in the barn walls as their eyes became used to the dark. Below them, the cattle moved in their pens. All around them was the drip drip drip of the rain from the barn roof.

"How do you like it?" Dan asked sleepily.

"This is just about the best thing to happen yet," Kip said. "Wait till I tell Edna I slept in a barn!"

"Happy birthday, anyway," Dan said.

Kip sat bolt upright. "My birthday? Is today the twenty-second?"

"It sure is. I knew you'd forgotten all about it. I remember your father saying when it was when you got Scout. Mine's next month and you won't catch me forgetting!"

Kip laughed. "That's the first time I've ever forgotten my birthday. Zowie! I'm twelve years old!" He listened suddenly. "What's that?"

Dan sat up, too. "It sounds like music."

"Music in a barn? It must be the cowbell."

"No, I'm not fooling, Kip. Listen," Dan said.

"Gosh, it's violins!" Kip exclaimed. "There's no radio out here, is there?"

A flash of light lit up their barn bedroom as the loft door was raised. A hand rose clutching a red lantern. A burst of fiddle music flowed up behind it. Dan and Kip stood up in astonishment.

"Surprise!" Bill shouted. Behind him came Milt, Sam and Joe, the first two with fiddles, the last with an accordion.

"Are you musicians?" Dan asked.

"We try to be," Milt said. "The Jimson Brothers and their old-time music." He bowed before the boys. "Would you like to hear a tune?"

"Would we!" Kip whooped. "Do you play before an audience and everything?"

"Sure thing," Bill said, "at the Hastings pavilion and anywhere else that wants us. Settle down now and we'll give you a concert."

In the next half hour the barn rang with old-time country dances. Kip found his foot beating time on the hay to the infectious rhythm. Later the brothers played three songs that they all sang together. "You'd better come along as our vocalists," Sam joked. "At your age kids' voices are usually changing gears but not yours."

"Time for sleep!" Joe announced. "You fellows have got a river to navigate tomorrow."

With a chorus of good nights the men disappeared through the loft door. Darkness took hold again and the boys stretched out on the hay.

"You know what, Dan?" Kip said.

"No, what, Champ?"

"This has been the best birthday I've ever had in my whole life!"

Dan laughed. "I bet it'll be the only one you'll spend in a barn, anyway." He turned over on his side. "We'd better get some sleep. Now that you're twelve I'll expect twice as much paddling out of you as I ever got before!"

14. A High Wind and An Accident

Kip was awakened in the morning by the distant rattle of a milk pail. He opened his eyes slowly and looked for Dan. He was gone. Kip jumped up, pulling the blanket after him. "Dan!" Then he saw his friend and began to laugh. In his sleep he had slid down to the bottom of the loft on the hay. He was almost hidden by it.

Dan heard him. Startled, he looked up at Kip. "Gosh, what happened to me? No wonder I was dreaming about shooting the rapids!"

"You must have been working at it hard," Kip said. "Listen! I hear somebody coming. Dive under the hay and pretend we're not here!"

Quickly they covered themselves and the blankets with hay. The loft door creaked and they heard a whistle, then Bill's voice. "Hey, Sam, they've taken wings. Too bad, eh, when Mary's whipping up a batch of waffles for breakfast."

Sam's deep tones echoed from the lower floor. "Better get

to work with the hay fork up there, Bill, to move some of that stuff down."

Two heads adorned with wisps of hay shot out of their hiding-place. "Not while we're in it, you don't!" Dan shouted. "Who'd miss waffles?"

Bill sat at the edge of the loft door dangling his long legs. "I thought that'd bring you to. How'd you sleep?"

"Super!" Kip peered through a crack in the barn wall. "Gee, it's hardly light yet."

"Up with the rooster on this farm, pal," Bill said. "Anyway, the rain's all gone and you've got a real day to travel."

"Is it good?" Dan shuffled through the hay to a door in the barn wall. When he flung it open cool northwest air flowed into the loft. "That's perfect," he said. "No more rain in sight for a while now."

"We'd better make an early start," Kip said. "I think I'll feel better paddling today."

It was half-past seven when the canoe was taken from its mooring in the creek. Protected by the heavy ground sheets, their equipment was sound and dry.

"Happy landings! Safe journey!"

"Come in a cruiser the next time and take us with you!"

"If you need a job we'll be waiting for you!"

The shouts echoed over the water as the boys saluted their hosts with the paddles. Then they turned their attention to the river. Glancing back Kip saw the four brothers swinging up the cow path towards the barn. "Do you think we'll ever see them again?" he said.

"Maybe," Dan said. "Let's hope so."

The morning was fresh and new. Everything, trees, river, cottages, stood out with the clarity of sculpture. A flock of ducks, their wings beating a rhythm, rose from a bed of reeds. High above, a meadow lark sang, the liquid notes rising and falling with the rise and fall of the paddles.

Within thirty minutes they were in sight of lock eighteen at

Hastings. Even before they rounded the bend in the river the boys could hear the throb of water at the dam. On the far bank an old stone mill crumbled into ruins and beside it, the water tumbled over shelves of craggy rock to the river below.

"Not too many people about yet," Dan said. "Let's tie up and wait for the store to open. We're going to need some more milk and canned goods, and a new axe."

Kip looked towards the bridge. "There are some men fishing. Why don't we give it a try?"

"It's all right with me."

They made the line secure and finding the tackle made off for the bridge. By the time the store had opened Dan had caught two fish. The storekeeper offered to give them a chunk of ice and some newspaper to keep them from the heat of the sun. "Although I don't think it's going to get too hot for them today," he added. "If it had been yesterday you'd have had to eat them right away!"

"We'll have to have company for lunch," Dan joked. "We'll never eat all of these."

When they were ready to go through the lock, a cruiser went with them, and other pleasure craft began to come to life on the river. By the time they reached the village of Trent River eight miles away, the water was humming with activity. Two sets of bridges crossed the river at this point and the views on both sides were wide and splendid. The river channel was dotted with wooded isles, the water flowing deep and blue and placid.

"Time for lunch, I guess," Dan said. "Would you like to eat in the restaurant or in the park?"

"There's the fish," Kip said. "Do you think it will be all right till supper?"

"Sure," Dan answered. "I'd like to find a good camp-site and have a real meal like we had on Spook Island."

"Okay." Kip stretched out his hand to catch at the rope on the cement wall. "Let's eat beside the canal." He stared up at the stern of the cruiser parked just in front of them. "Boy!" he added. "That's a real boat."

It was a massive affair of white and gray with a thin red line dividing the two tones. A name sparkled in gold on the prow. Brass shone up on the deck and wide glass windows glistened, reflecting the river.

"Christopher!"

Kip looked up with a start. Someone was calling him from the deck. He shaded his eyes against the sun. A man of more than ordinary size was leaning his plump body against the deck rail staring down at the boys. He was almost bald and the flesh about his chin and eyes hung in thick folds of fat. "How did you get here?" he asked.

"We've come down from Lakefield!" Kip called. "We started on Saturday!" He spoke in a low tone to Dan. "It's Mr. Hendry, a business friend of my father's."

They watched while Mr. Hendry turned to speak to someone in the cabin. Then he returned to the rail. "Come up and have lunch with us," he said.

Kip glanced quickly at Dan. "We'd like that very much." He noticed the big man hesitate and once again refer to the unseen person in the cabin.

"Doesn't your guide have something to eat down there?" he asked. "He'd rather eat outside, anyway, wouldn't he?"

"Dan's not my guide, Mr. Hendry." Kip was surprised to hear his own voice so firm and sure of itself. "I think we'd both better eat over on the wall. It's such a fine day." He gazed steadily at the man. "Thank you very much for the invitation." Then he turned to the task of tying up and pretended to busy himself with the duffle. When he looked up again the man had disappeared into the cabin.

Kip cast an apologetic glance towards Dan. He did not know what to say.

Dan smiled his slow smile. "Forget it, Champ," he said. "You know what I told you. It takes all kinds." He helped Kip to find the food. "You said he was a business friend of your father's. Won't your dad be angry with you?"

"My father will be angry with him," Kip told him, and they said no more about it.

On their way to Heely Falls islands dotted the blue water. "There's one I thought you might like to spend the night on, Kip!" said Dan, pointing.

"Why?" Kip asked.

"Because it's called Haunted Island!"

"Sure," said Kip. "That's just our style."

"Don't worry, pal," Dan said, "one of those is enough on any trip. I was just pulling your leg."

They put into shore for an hour to enjoy a swim from a secluded inlet on the left bank and then moved on. As their canoe approached the narrowing channel that carried them into Heely Falls Kip shouted, "Listen! You can hear the water roaring even from here!"

"No wonder," Dan said. "There's a big drop here. Below the dam the water falls into a huge deep gorge."

When they came in sight of the docks, several small power boats and a large cruiser were already moored there. "We can't stay here too long," Dan warned. "We have to push on and find a good camp-site for the night."

They made camp at seven beside the ruins of an old mill. They poked about among the stones but the inside was shrouded with dust and they were afraid to go in for fear of rotting floor-boards. They were off again down river in the gray light of morning before the sun was up.

At eight they pulled in to the shore, ravenously hungry. "You want to eat up all the supplies before we come to the next store?" Dan asked as Kip started on his fourth piece of toast.

"Well, I was only trying to help," Kip said in the same bantering tone. "The canoe will be lighter to paddle if I do."

"But you won't!" Dan pointed out. "And if you don't watch

out, I'm going to have to get you new clothes before we finish this trip. The others won't fit any more."

"Okay, then I'll travel in my bathing trunks," Kip laughed. "At least they stretch!"

Dan was watching the sky. "You know," he said, "something is happening to the weather again. Can you feel it?"

"It seems warmer all of a sudden, doesn't it?"

"Uh-huh." Dan pointed to a thickening blanket of high cloud. "That means more rain, I'll bet. I just wonder when."

"We don't really care, do we?" Kip said. "We didn't make out so badly the last time."

"No, but I was hoping the good weather would last for a couple of days," Dan said. "The warm air is coming in awfully fast." He held up his arms to the wind. "That breeze is getting pretty strong, too. Do you think you can keep us midstream against that?"

"I don't think I'll have any trouble." Kip spoke confidently but once on their way again the gusts became stronger, blowing them in towards the right shore.

Dan sensed Kip's uncertainty. "Don't let it worry you." He had to shout hard above the wind. "Keep your head and watch where you're going and I'll do the rest. If it gets too bad we'll put in and stay for the day."

It was not that the wind grew worse, but that he failed to keep his mind strictly on the business at hand. As the canoe was gliding past a company of rocks, a heron rose from a creek on the opposite shore. The huge body, long legs dangling, astonished Kip with its large wing-spread, and he stared. It was only a moment but it was long enough. Dan was driving the canoe from the stern with such force that Kip's failure to respond at the bow sent it spinning in towards the rocks. The wind leaped at it fiercely, and in an instant the canoe overturned and the boys were struggling in the water. There was no need for panic. The water was deep but they were out of midstream, the only spot where the current was swift. Kip, as he clung to the craft, saw their gear sink to the bottom.

"Get the canoe into shore!" Dan shouted. "We'll worry about the rest later!"

Flailing the water with their legs they pushed and tugged the canoe towards the bank. There was a sudden scraping sound.

"Careful!" Dan warned. "It's on a rock! Take it easy from here on in. We should be able to touch bottom soon."

In another moment Kip felt ground under his feet. "Ouch!" he gasped. "It's all stony."

"Bear up, pal. We have to get this thing up on shore," Dan said. "Make it snappy or the current will carry all our gear away."

They struggled across the rocks and deposited the canoe in the high grasses on the bank. "Come on," Dan shouted. "Are you ready to help?"

"Sure!" Kip said."Let's go!"

They drove down to where the duffle was imprisoned by rocks. Taking it a little at a time, surfacing frequently for breath, they managed to tug the two large bundles into the shallow water.

"Jeepers!" Dan said. "Are we lucky! That stuff could have been sailing down to Lake Ontario right now if it hadn't been for those rocks!"

Kip was winded. He sat breathing deeply. "Well, that's our first accident," he said at last, "and it was all my fault."

"What do you mean your fault?"

"I was watching that silly heron, wasn't I? If I'd been paying attention to what I was doing, it would never have happened." He lay back in the grasses, his sodden clothes squelching.

"If it was anybody's fault it was mine," Dan said. "I should have known enough not to try to go on in this wind. Say, I'll bet you're cold," he added.

"Kind of shivery," Kip said.

"Thank goodness for that oilskin case," Dan said. "We'll be able to build a fire." He grinned. "This reminds me of the storm at Hastings, except that we went down to meet the water this time instead of it coming down to meet us!"

The shore at this point was lined with a column of trees, mostly hardwoods, and they had no trouble finding fuel among the broken branches in the grass. Dan brought stones from the water's edge to make a wind-shield, and soon had a fire blazing behind them. The boys nestled in the hollow, their clothes strung like scarecrows on sticks. The wind and the fire did not take long to do their work and they were soon in dry clothing again, arranging the rest of the equipment before the heat of the flames.

"I'm cold," said Kip. "Let's dry the wind-breaker first and then I can put it on."

"Where is it?" Dan asked.

"Oh gosh," Kip said. "Now we've had it."

"What do you mean?"

"I had it folded up behind me when I was paddling. That means it's gone down the river, and my wallet was in the pocket!"

"Oh, brother!" Dan sat down suddenly. "Well, that's that, I guess. Let's see what I've got." He pulled the sodden wallet from his jeans pocket. "This is pretty wet but it's still money. But it isn't enough to buy a wind-breaker for you and pay for supplies till we get home. We're nearly out of everything. I was counting on picking up quite a bit of stuff in Campbellford."

Kip jumped up. "Dan, why couldn't we get a job?"

"There's no reason why we can't," Dan said. "There must be somebody looking for help around a big place like Campbellford. Okay, Champ, let's load up and be ready to get going in case the wind drops."

The great gusts had died down within another hour. The breeze was still strong but not enough to hinder their going. They arrived in Campbellford three-quarters of an hour later, clinging close to the right shore. They were approaching a makeshift dock where a woman sat knitting, watching three small children in the water. The woman waved at them as they came close. "Hello!" she called. "Having a good trip?"

"Let's ask her," Dan said. "She probably lives here all year round and knows the place really well." He paddled in to the dock.

"Hi," he said. "We're having a fine time, thanks. Do you know anywhere we could get a job in this place?"

"A job?" The woman came down the dock to its edge. "What do you want a job for?"

"Oh, we had a little accident back up the river a piece," Dan said, "and we lost a wallet. We hate to call home for money at this stage in the game."

The three children splashed around the canoe and the woman ordered them away. "An accident!" she said. "Are you both all right?"

"Sure," Kip said. "All right except for money."

"And that can be pretty important when you haven't got any," the woman smiled. "The only place I know of is the new restaurant they're building on the river about half a mile down. Why don't you put in here and go down to see if you can find the owner?"

"If you're sure you don't mind," Dan said.

"I don't mind at all. In fact, if you can get a job you can sleep over the boat-house if you'd like to. My name is Mrs. Wallace and these are my children, Kerry, Joyce and Jeff."

The boys introduced themselves and paddled the canoe into the boat-house beside a small motor boat.

"Do you think we could eat before we start out?" Kip asked. "I'm starved!"

"Come on up into the kitchen," Mrs. Wallace said, "and I'll make you a sandwich." And despite the boys' protests that they had canned stuff in the canoe, she insisted upon it. Half an hour later they were on their way into town.

15. Scout's Gone!

The main street was quiet in the early afternoon. There was little business doing in the stores. "Saturday's the big day in these places," Dan said. "The farmers all come in then and people are either coming or going from the summer cottages."

They saw the large lift bridge crossing the river and the two railway bridges, and then they came in view of the building site. It was laid down on a smooth stretch of greensward bordering the river bank. It was evidently intended for both road and river traffic for a ramp led down to the water and a series of window openings looked down upon it, and there were openings in the face of the place towards the road.

"There's hope for us," Dan said. "They haven't done the roof yet. I wonder where we go to ask."

"What do you two kids want around here?"

They turned to find a tall coarse-featured man standing behind them. "Well," he said, "what are you looking for, a hand-out?"

"No, sir," Dan replied. "We're looking for a job."

"What can you do that brings you here? We don't want any kids working for us."

"We can do carpentry," Kip burst in. "I helped my dad build our summer cottage and Dan's been working with his father for years."

"I'll believe that when I see it," the man said. He stared at them coldly. "I think you'd better get on your way out of here."

"At least you could give us a chance," Dan protested. "That wouldn't do you any harm, would it?"

The man frowned. "Not if I keep an eye on you, I guess." He glanced up at the building. "We could do with some help on that roof before the rain comes. Every Tom Dick and Harry is away on holidays right now." He moved towards a little booth beyond the new building. "I'll speak to the boss," he called over his shoulder.

"I wonder who the boss is," Kip whispered.

They saw him in a minute, a very plump black-haired man in a white apron who came to the window of the booth. While they talked the boys could hear the broken English of the plump man above the husky voice of the other.

"I think he's Italian," Kip said. "Maybe he'll be more friendly than the other fellow."

The first man came back in a moment. "He says it's okay with him. All he wants is to get the job done. But you'd better not try any tricks because I'll be right there to watch you."

"When do you want us to start?" Dan asked.

"Tomorrow morning. I'll be here at eight. You be here then, too, if you want the job. I'll pay you forty cents an hour and not a penny more." With that the man turned on his heel and left.

"Nice type," Dan said with a grin. "But what do we care as long as we get paid! Forty cents an hour should see us through all right."

"What shall we do this afternoon?" Kip asked.

"We'd better get back and spread some more of our gear out to dry before it rains," Dan said. "Then, you know what?"

"No, what?" Kip said.

"I think we should squander some money on a movie. There's one in town."

"Oh, boy! What's playing tonight?" Kip said.

"A sea picture. I saw the sign when we came by." Dan laughed. "Unless you've had enough water for one day."

"Not me," said Kip. "Let's go!"

They spent a pleasant afternoon by the river telling the Wallace family their adventures and diving with them off the dock. At Mrs. Wallace's insistence, they stayed for supper.

When they came out of the movie at nine-thirty the wind had dropped completely and a gentle slow rain was falling. "Dan," Kip said, "what happens to our job tomorrow if it rains?"

"Don't worry," Dan said, "it may have stopped by morning." It had stopped by the time they reached the boat-house. They turned on the flashlight to discover that Mrs. Wallace had left some extra blankets and two pillows.

"This is really roughing it," Dan laughed. "What would Dad say if he saw those pillows?"

"We may need them before morning," Kip said. "There aren't any pine branches around here and that floor looks awfully hard to me!"

When Dan shook Kip awake at six-thirty in the morning, the sun was shining through the cracks in the boat-house wall. "Get up, Champ," Dan said. "We'll have a swim, and then we'll head for breakfast in town."

"What a perfect morning for putting on a roof!" Kip said.

"Don't be so sure," Dan said. "It's going to be pretty hot up there in that blazing sun."

In the town a train was shunting back and forth across the railway bridge and two tourist cars passed, laden from roof to wheel. Otherwise all was quiet. To their dismay they found that the restaurant was closed. They crossed over to the Chinese café. Its door, too, was locked and the window shade pulled to the floor.

"Now what?" Kip groaned. "I'm starved after that dip."

"Me, too," Dan said. "Maybe we can get something from the booth next to the job when it opens."

They were waiting at the building at a quarter to eight, and the man arrived on the dot fifteen minutes later. He gave them a curt nod and told them where to find their tools. "The name's Mills," he said. "But don't be bothering me with a lot of questions. Either you know how to do the job or you don't, and if you don't you can get on your way."

"Okay," Dan said. "We'll be all right. There's nothing much to a straight job of shingling."

By the middle of the morning Kip was so hungry that he could scarcely keep going. "The booth's open," he whispered to Dan as he reached for more nails. "I saw the Italian man go in half an hour ago. Do you think we dare ask if we can go?"

"Sure," Dan said. "I'm game." He crawled across the roof to where Mr. Mills was working on the other side. "Sir," he said, "Could we go down just for a second to grab a bite to eat at the booth?"

The man stared at him. "Just what I thought. You're just like all the other kids, wanting something for nothing."

Kip saw Dan's lips set in a firm line. "It isn't that, Mr. Mills," he said. "The restaurants were closed this morning so we couldn't get anything to eat. We'll be back in a minute. Honest."

"See that it's no longer, that's all." The man bent to his task and did not look at them again.

"Yippee! Food!" Dan said. "Come on, let's go!"

They scrambled quickly to the ground. While they gulped their hamburgers and milk the man at the booth, smiling and friendly, told them how he had had the booth for five years and saved enough to build the restaurant. "My family come from Italy soon," he confided. "My wife, Maria, three boys and two girls." He pointed to the roof. "He build da place for me. Good builder."

"It's just as well there's something good about him," Dan whispered as they clambered up on the roof. "It sure isn't his disposition."

Mr. Mills came to inspect their work a short time later. The boys did not stop hammering while he probed along the shingles they had already done. "It'll do," he said at last. "Lunch hour's at twelve noon and just make sure you're back on the job at one sharp."

"Okay, sir," Dan said.

"Gee, what a grouch!" Kip whispered. "I think we're doing a super job myself!"

"I don't think he's sorry he hired us, anyway," Dan said.

The sun blazed all morning in a clear sky. Even the nails in the pail between them grew warm to touch. "I don't need to worry about a burn any more, anyway," Kip said, flinging off his shirt. "But I wish we could work in our bathing-suits."

"Tomorrow we'll put them on under our jeans and go in for a dip at noon," Dan suggested.

They both laid down their hammers thankfully when the noon whistle blew.

"Now I know how a hot dog must feel," Dan grinned.

Kip began to scramble down the roof. "I've been dreaming up a great big dishful of ice cream all morning. Have we got enough money to buy some?"

"Sure." Dan glanced up the river. "Boy! There's a nice boat coming down-stream. How would you like to be sitting on deck there with your feet up?"

"That would suit me just fine," Kip said, "and I'd tell the butler to bring me a double helping of ice-cold lemonade." He took a quick second look. "Dan, I know that boat!"

"Oh?" Dan sat still on the roof edge. "Jeepers! So do I! It's that one we met at Lakefield at the start of the trip. What was the name?"

"The *Eldora* from Rochester!" Kip began to wave wildly to the three people on deck. Suddenly they saw him and began to wave back. "Come on, let's go down and see them!" he shouted.

They hurried down to the retaining wall and waited while the cruiser thudded gently against the protective bumpers. The man with the crew cut leaned over the rail. "Well," he called, "what are you two doing here? I thought you'd be well ahead of us. We've just been loafing along."

"That's one thing we're not doing," Dan laughed. "We got into a little trouble and we're working our way out of it, that's all."

"Come on up and tell us what happened," the man said.

The boys went aboard and the man introduced himself, his wife and daughter. His name was Morgan and he was a doctor. "Now tell us your names and what's happened to you," he said.

The boys told the story of the canoe upset and the job. "But you can't work up on that roof in this dreadful heat," Mrs. Morgan objected. "You're liable to come down with sunstroke."

"It is a little warm," Dan smiled. "But we'll live."

"Why don't you call your parents and have them bring you some money?" Mrs. Morgan asked. "Or better still let us lend you some?"

"Oh, no, thank you, we'll manage," Kip said.

"Where are you two boys staying?" Dr. Morgan asked.

"In the loft of a boat-house," Kip said. They told him about Mrs. Wallace's hospitality.

"The heat up there is going to be pretty insufferable to-night," the doctor said. "Why don't you come and join us? We have two sleeping-bags. You can settle down on the deck."

"Come right after work and have supper with us," Mrs.

Morgan said. "By that time I'll have figured out a way to get you off that roof."

Kip glanced at Dan. "I'd sure like that," he said.

"Me, too. Thanks a lot," Dan said. "We'll let Mrs. Wallace know right now where we're going to be."

They picked up their things at the boat-house after they had eaten. Even then the air in the loft was stifling. At one, on the roof, it was no better. At three Mr. Mills appeared on the roof ridge. "You kids better knock off and get a drink," he said. "But see that you don't take all day."

"Boy! What a relief!" Dan said. "I was just about going up in a puff of smoke!"

"What I wouldn't do for a swim right about now!" Kip sighed, as they drank their pop.

"Hold on, Champ," Dan said. "It won't be long now, and you can have one. Three hours to go."

At Mrs. Morgan's suggestion, they swam from the cruiser deck before supper. "Now you look better," Mrs. Morgan smiled. "Sit down and enjoy yourselves and tell us all your adventures."

Over sizzling steaks and apple pie the boys told their story. When they came to the part about the man chasing them from the camp-site Mrs. Morgan looked indignant. "I'd like to have a word or two with that gentleman," she said. "Whatever was the matter with him?"

Kip was surprised at Dan's frankness before them. "Oh, it was me, I guess," he said. "In some places Indians aren't too well thought of."

"It's probably because people in general don't know anything about them," the doctor said. "They can't get to know you very well when you live on Reserves. But after all, Indians had a great deal to do with the development of this country, didn't they?"

"Indians?" Kip said, surprised. "How?"

"When the French first came here they came from a land of

roads and highways. It was the Indian who showed them how to travel in the wilderness. It was the Indian dress of fur and moose-skin that the early explorers adopted. And what about food? It was the Indian maize and beans, corn and pumpkin and squash that the settlers first planted and ate." Dr. Morgan smiled at Dan. "And right now you're guiding your friend here down an old Indian trail. Dozens of highways in your country and mine are laid over old Indian routes."

"Never mind about all that now," Mrs. Morgan put in. "I've finally decided how we can help these boys."

"But Mary," the doctor said, "the boys evidently don't think they need help."

"Well, I do," she said. "I'm sure their mothers would be horrified to know what's happened. I think they should come down the canal with us."

"With you?" Dan said.

"Why not?" Mrs. Morgan said. "You can tie on at our stern and sleep on the deck as you're going to do tonight."

The doctor laughed. "It seems to me I suggested at the start of the trip that you might like a hitch-hike. My wife seems sure of it now."

"It's sure nice of you to ask us," Dan said. He looked at Kip.

"We couldn't do that, thanks all the same," Kip said. "We still have a lot of things to do. We'll make out all right. Thanks again." He thought of the blazing sun on the roof the next day and of Mr. Mills, and wondered if he had said the right thing. But there were still nights ahead under the stars with Dan, and a trip to Stirling for Edna. It was worth it all to have these.

The moon shone, pale and new, from a cloudless starlit sky when the doctor and his wife went below. Kip did not fall asleep at once, tired as he was with the day on the roof. Laughter and splashing told him that someone nearby was enjoying a night swim, and far off, down the river, he heard the hum of a power boat. Then a dog began to bark and he thought of

Scout. He tried to picture him lying on the verandah at Kip's Cove, the big powerful body stretched out full on the mat, the head between the large paws, the eyes open, watching, alert. Perhaps even now he was facing the door waiting for Kip to come home. Thinking of the dog waiting for him, he fell asleep.

They were up before the sun in the morning, taking an early swim. Breakfast was an appetizing affair of pancakes and sausages eaten on the open deck. "You won't think much of my cooking after this," Dan said to Kip.

"You could have pancakes for breakfast all the way home," Mrs. Morgan reminded them. "Just come along as I suggested."

But the boys had made up their minds. They were up on the roof again, hammering away at the shingles in a heat that was already intense when the cruiser pulled up its moorings and they stood to wave good-bye. By two in the afternoon Kip wished that he had not been so hasty in saying no to Mrs. Morgan. He did not know how he could go on. The morning had been bad enough, but the air on the roof after lunch was like that of a blast furnace. It was all he could do to curb his tongue when Mr. Mills crawled down the slope to see them an hour later. "Get going, you kids," he ordered. "You're slowing up, and I want this job done by the time you leave tonight."

"We want it done, too," Dan said pleasantly. "We'd like to be on the river again tomorrow morning."

Mr. Mills made no move to go. He stood staring down at them. It made Kip feel even more uncomfortable. Then he spoke again. "You kids come from Bloomfield way?"

Dan and Kip looked up in surprise. "How did you know?" Kip said.

"There's been somebody trying to get you on the telephone." Kip gaped at Dan. "Oh, oh! What day is today?"

"Friday," said Dan. "We forgot all about the telephone call."

"The woman up at central has told everybody on the river

to look out for you," Mr. Mills said shortly. "There's been a message there since this morning."

"What kind of a message?" Kip asked.

"You're to put a call through to Operator twenty-one on long distance," Mr. Mills said, "at seven tonight." He made off up the roof calling over his shoulder, "And don't be skipping off trying to do it now."

"Mr. Mills," Dan shouted, "if we hurry it up and finish the job by five, do you mind if we leave then? We want to buy some supplies before the stores close."

"It's all right with me," Mr. Mills said, "but you'll never make it."

Kip stared after him. "Jeepers Creepers, Mom will be worried sick."

"I know," Dan said, "but it's no wonder we forgot, with the accident and everything."

"I wish we could call right now."

"It wouldn't be any good, even if we could leave the job," Dan said. "Your father won't be up at the store till seven. Come on now, Champ, let's pour the work on and show the boss we can make it. We have to get your wind-breaker and some stuff to eat."

Between his concern at forgetting the phone call and the effort to be finished, the heat took second place in his thoughts for the rest of the afternoon. They hammered the last nail in at ten after five. Mr. Mills would not pay them until the entire job was given his approval. "I'll dock you for the hour," he said. "You aren't working till six."

Dan was about to speak, then closed his mouth. He forced a smile as he took the money. "Thanks for the job, anyway," he said. "We appreciated it."

"Gee," Kip said as they moved off, "and after we slaved to get it done!"

"Oh, never mind," Dan said. "We've got lots here for the wind-breaker and the food. That's the important thing."

"Let's celebrate by having a bang-up meal in a restaurant when we've been to the stores," Kip said. "We'll have to stay around down here to get to a pay phone at seven."

"It's okay with me," Dan said. "Heat or not, I could eat a horse."

The wind-breaker was cheap, on sale in an end of summer clearance, and they had plenty left over for food supplies. The restaurant was very hot but Kip was too happy to have the job done to worry about it. He was glad that their affairs were now in order and he need mention no difficulty at all when he spoke to his father.

When the telephone call had been placed, Kip heard Mr. Bell announcing the store. Then he was pleased to hear his father's voice.

"Hello, Kip!"

"Hi, Dad! I'm sorry we forgot to call," Kip said. "I guess Mom wondered what happened!"

"We all did," Mr. Brooks said. "But Mother was pretty anxious. How are things going?"

"Wonderful, Dad! We had a tipping, but everything's okay now. Don't tell Mom about the tipping!"

"A tipping!" his father said. "Are you absolutely sure everything is all right?"

"Positive, Dad. Tell Mom everything's fine. How's Scout doing, Dad? Do you think he misses me?"

There was only silence for a moment.

"Dad, how's Scout?" Kip repeated. "I can't wait to get home to see him again."

"Kip," his father said. "I was hoping you wouldn't ask right now. Scout's gone."

"Gone!" Kip could not believe it. "Gone where?"

"I don't know, son. Edna had him out for a run two days ago and he made off and he never came back."

"Dad, he just couldn't go! He must be around there somewhere!"

"We've looked everywhere, Kip," his father said. "We even went up to the Reserve to see if somehow he'd got back there. We just haven't been able to find him, but we're still looking."

Kip said nothing. He could think of nothing to say.

"Kip," his father said.

"Yes, Dad?"

"Don't be too upset, he may come back yet. I didn't really want you to find out until you came home."

"It's okay, Dad," Kip said. "Thanks, anyway." He could feel the big lump in his throat. He felt like crying but you didn't cry when you're twelve years old.

"Don't worry now," Mr. Brooks was saying, "he may come back yet, and if he doesn't we'll get you another dog as soon as you get home."

"But I don't want another dog," Kip thought. "I want Scout. He was the best dog anybody ever had." He said, "I guess I better go now, Dad, Dan's waiting for me."

"Mr. Bell said to call here when you get into Trenton and he'll get the message to us," Mr. Brooks told him. "Shall I give your love to your mother and Edna?"

"Sure," Kip said. "I'll see you, Dad." And then he hung up.

Dan had been listening. He did not have to be told what had happened. "Don't worry, Champ," he said, "he may come back."

"I don't think he will," Kip said. "I didn't have him long enough to really get to know him. He didn't know how much I liked him. He's gone somewhere looking for old Len, and I'll never see him again."

"Kip," Dan said, "would you like to go home right now, straight home, I mean?"

That's what he would have liked to have done. Gone straight home and roamed the woods and fields for miles around, whistling and calling the dog's name. He felt somehow that if he were there the dog would know and come back. But Dan had counted on this trip. It was his summer holiday and he had asked Kip to enjoy it with him. He could not let Dan down now.

"No," he said, "I want to finish the trip. I won't talk about him, I promise. I'll try to forget the whole thing."

But later, as they lay waiting for sleep to come in the heat of the boat-house loft, the dog was all he could think about. He remembered the feel of the rough tongue cold on his cheek, and the shining coat coarse to his hand. He remembered the races up the beach and the strength of the lithe body as it lunged at him in play.

"What's the matter?" Dan asked. "Are you too hot to sleep?"

"It is pretty warm," Kip said, "but there's nothing we can do about that."

"You bet there is," Dan said. "Let's go in for a swim. Then we can take our blankets out and sleep on the lawn."

The water felt wonderful to their hot tired bodies. "I don't even feel at all sleepy now," Kip said, when they spread the blankets under the big willow by the shore. But just the same his eyes closed as soon as he put his head to the ground.

The sun was shining through the tree branches, dappling the grass around him with light, when he awoke. He remembered that there was something unpleasant to be thought of, and then he remembered the dog. With a determined effort he put it out of his mind and sat up.

"Hi," Dan said. He was rearranging some duffle in the canoe. "We can take our time getting away this morning. There are two locks to go through, which is one too many to portage. I'm lazy."

"Me, too," Kip said. He took a deep breath. "Dan, it doesn't seem so hot this morning."

"It isn't," Dan agreed. "There isn't half as much humidity as yesterday. It'll be good travelling weather."

"We should go up before we leave and thank Mrs. Wallace," Kip suggested.

"Sure," Dan said. "She's been a real pal, letting us use this place."

She appeared on the lawn a few moments later. "You had the right idea, sleeping out here," she said. "We all should have come and joined you." She lifted her tanned face to the breeze. "Mmm, that's cooler today. There's a good breakfast inside. Could I interest anybody?"

"Thanks all the same," Dan said, "but we're counting on making a fire a few miles down the river."

"It seems a long time since we've had one," Kip said.

"Take care the rest of the journey, won't you?" she warned. "I'll be thinking of you. I have some cookies up at the house for you to put in your tuck bag."

"You sound like our Edna," Kip grinned. And when he thought of her he wished she were here right now so that he could tell her how he felt about Scout. Edna would understand. He always told Edna everything.

Mrs. Wallace and the three children were on the dock when the boys left, waving and waving until they lost sight of one another.

Kip glanced back up the river once for a farewell glimpse of the town. It hugged the river shores, quiet in the morning sun. He had left something of himself there in a new roof on the river bank, and he had left, too, a dream of companionship with the best dog that anybody could ever have.

16. Kanati, Lucky Hunter

They put into shore a short distance beyond lock eleven for their breakfast. It was good to be eating out in the open again, with the snapping of the fire and the sound of the birds all around them. "We're really eating fancy this morning," Dan said. "Sausages with our bacon and eggs, and iced buns with the milk."

"We must be celebrating," Kip said. But there isn't much to celebrate, he thought.

"Sure," Dan said. "We're celebrating a wallet full of money we earned ourselves and a new wind-breaker. And anyway, it's good to be on the river again."

Yes, Kip thought, it is good, if only he could put Scout out of his mind. There was still the wonder of what they might find around the next bend in the river, and all the joys of camping out. If only Scout had not gone.

"It won't be long now till Stirling," Dan said, poking the fire. "You still want to go?"

"Sure," Kip said. "Edna's told me so much about it I wouldn't want to miss that place."

As he remembered, all his young childhood days had been filled with Edna's tales of the town. Edna was never without a story as long as she had her old home town to talk about. There was the mill pond where she swam every summer and skated every winter. Kip recalled the story of the day her younger brother had fallen through the ice and nearly drowned. There was the crusty old man who at one time had owned the feed-and-grain shop, and how he had awakened on the morning following one Hallowe'en to find an ancient hooded buggy on top of his roof. Kip had always suspected that Edna had had a great deal to do with putting it there. She had often told him of the memorial park and of the time she won first prize in elocution there at the school fair, and of the long steep, maple-lined street, too, where she and her brothers tobogganed one moonlit night, because they were forbidden to do so in the day-time. Edna had declared that it was worth the spanking they all got when they reached home. There had been taffy pulls and sleigh-rides and fowl suppers, all the things that Kip wished he could have done himself. And now of course, there was Edna's ghost.

"Dan, do you really believe in ghosts?" Kip asked.

"Not a bit," Dan said. Then he grinned quickly. "But that's easy to say in the broad daylight, isn't it?" He glanced at Kip. "What's the matter, Champ? Are you thinking about Edna's ghost story?"

"Yes," Kip confessed, "but I guess it's just a story." He thought of the voice in the night calling the Indian name up and down the corridors of an old stone house.

"It'll be fun to see the old house, anyway," Dan said. "We'll be able to tell Edna."

Suddenly Kip could not wait to be there. "Let's get going," he said, leaping up. "We've got miles to cover."

A mile and a half farther they came upon the solid land

mass of Meyers Island in midstream and chose the channel on their left, passing another island on their way to the next lock.

In late morning they pulled in to watch two sailboats racing in a wide lovely sweep of the river as it bent eastward. The channel was heavily buoyed beyond this point and there were large areas of marshy swamp. They had lunch on Hickory Island. There seemed to be no one about as they ate in the still sunshine beside the water, but it was a different story in mid-afternoon. They were making steady progress along the neck of water that separates the large bulk of Wilson Island and the southern mainland, when they saw a fleet of canoes bearing down upon them.

"Boy Scouts!" Dan cried out. "It's a camping trip!"

They hove to and exchanged greetings. "We've just left a fine camp-site over there on the island," the Scoutmaster told them. "If you're not in a hurry, why don't you put in there for the night? We've even left you a pile of firewood."

"Good idea," Dan said. "We're ready for a swim, anyway."

They watched the Scouts bearing away up the river. "That's a nice bunch," said Dan. "Too bad we couldn't have all camped together."

"Sure," Kip said, but he was glad that they had not. Time on this trip was running out now, and his nights under the stars with Dan were numbered. Maybe it was mean to want Dan all to himself, but that's the way he liked it.

"Okay with you if we camp here?" Dan asked.

"It looks fine to me. I was wondering when we were going to get a swim."

It did not take them long to unload the supplies near the stack of firewood, and to race into the water. A large cruiser spun past and they had fun diving into the waves it left behind. It was time for supper when they came out of the river, ravenous.

Afterwards Dan took Kip for a hike through the woods,

pointing out wild shrubs and giving him some elements of woodcraft. "How would you like a little music?" Dan asked as they wandered back to camp.

"Music?" Kip said. "What are we going to do, whistle?" "Old Len taught me how to make an Indian flute once," Dan said. "We'll both make one and have a concert."

Dusk came on as they sat whittling by the fire. When they were finished, the thin plaintive notes of the two flutes sounded sweet and clear in the darkness and stillness of the island. Dan taught Kip an Indian tune. It made a sad little song and reminded Kip of Scout again. He was glad when they turned to "Old MacDonald had a farm" and "Green grow the rushes O".

The moon tangled in the branches over their heads flooded the camp with silver. "If only we had old Len along," Kip said, "we could have a story right about now." *I wish it could be a story about Scout coming back, he thought, and it was all true.*

"I could tell you one he told me," Dan offered. "I won't say I'll make much of a job of it, but it'll be better than nothing."

"You didn't tell me you knew any stories," Kip said. "Get going! I'm waiting!"

"This story is called 'The Legend of Wild Boy'," Dan began, "and it's a story of our own people, the Iroquois. Thousands and thousands of years ago, when the world was just beginning, an Indian hunter, his wife and their little boy lived on the banks of a great river."

"That's a good beginning," Kip said, "when we're on a great river right now."

"The woman's name was Selu which means Indian corn, and the man's name was Kanati."

"So that's where you got the name for your canoe. I know what that means, lucky hunter!"

"That's right," Dan said. "This Kanati was a lucky hunter, too. Every day he went out to search for food and every day he managed to bring home more than enough for his family. His wife and son never asked how he came to be so lucky with the bow and arrow. They just took things as they came. But then something happened." Dan poked the fire and a shower of sparks lit the darkness. "One day, while she was cleaning the food at the river's edge, Selu heard her son talking to someone. 'Who is your friend?' she asked him. 'He is Wild Boy, and he lives in the river,' her son answered. 'Bring him home to see us,' Selu said. So he did, and they liked Wild Boy so much they invited him to come and live with them. Wild Boy was curious about the hunting ways of Kanati. He wondered what made him such a lucky hunter."

"Everybody says curiosity killed the cat," Kip said. "Did it this time?"

"Just about. He persuaded the son one day to go with him and follow Kanati when he went to search for food. They watched him come to a great stone before the mouth of a cave. When he rolled the stone away a short distance, out sprang a deer. Kanati killed the deer and set off home with it. The two boys wanted to do like the father, so they ran home to get their bows and arrows and back to the cave. Together they rolled the stone away from the cave and as they did, out came all the animals of the world, leaping, running, jumping, until the cave was empty. Kanati, who was skinning his catch at home, heard the sound of thunder on the earth and he knew something was wrong. He went in search of the boys. When he saw what they had done he said, 'This is the end of man's easy days of hunting. From this day forward, man will have to struggle to find his food, and even then he may not always find it.' Of course Wild Boy and the young son were sorry for the evil they had caused, but they couldn't do anything about it, and that's why today man must seek his food with much work and trouble, but it was not always so in the beginning of the world."

"I guess that's why, if I want a bun right now, I have to go and dig for it in the duffle," Kip said.

"Right," Dan grinned. "And bring me one, too, while you're at it. I'm hungry again."

When they were ready for sleep, Kip lay watching the glow of the fire and thinking about Len Big Canoe and the dog. What would become of Scout alone on the country roads and in the fields, trying to find his way to his old master? Old Len would be in Brantford by now, with his daughter. No dog would ever be able to travel all that distance. Was he lying behind some hedge now, ragged and hungry in the dark of night? He could not bear to think of him like that, not his Scout. He turned and buried his face in the blanket. Somewhere, somehow Scout must be found. It was not long now till home, and he could begin the search himself.

"Champ!" He felt Dan's foot nudge him.

"Yes?" He whispered as Dan had done, but he did not know why.

"Look, over there, on the other side of the fire."

Kip followed the pointing finger. Three shapes, one large and two smaller, moved in the half darkness. "What is it?" he asked.

"A porky and her young ones going down to the river for a drink."

Now he could see all the eyes gleaming in the dark. He watched the tiny procession disappear over the edge of the bank and waited. A few moments later the animals returned, lumbering slowly through the grasses to the silent, moonlit woods. Watching them, Kip fell asleep.

When he opened his eyes the next morning, Dan was still asleep. Creeping out of his blanket, he got the fire going and quietly set about making breakfast. Dan sat up with a start as the bacon began to sputter in the fry-pan. "Jeepers, this is a switch," he said. "Am I having my breakfast in bed this morning?"

"Sure," said Kip. "You're not the only one that can cook, you know."

"It smells good enough to me," Dan said. "We'd better build

up our strength this morning. Today's the day we go ghost-hunting."

"What time will we get to Stirling?" Kip asked, his mind leaping ahead to the mill pond and the tree-lined street and the great stone house with the white pillars.

"Search me," Dan answered. "I don't know whether we'll be able to paddle up the creek or not. We'll soon find out though."

"Are we starting right after we've eaten?"

"Let's not hurry," Dan said. "We're almost at the end of the journey and I'd like to make it last."

Kip said nothing. He was torn between excitement at the Stirling adventure and the deep urge to be home in search of his dog. "Gosh," he said, "school starts in another week. I just can't believe the holidays are nearly over."

"What grade will you be going into, Champ?" Dan asked.

"Grade eight. How about you?"

"I'll be going to high school this year." Dan toasted his bread on a stick over the flames. "It'll be more work, I guess, but I'm sure looking forward to the football and hockey and stuff."

"You're lucky," Kip said. "I wish I was going to high school." The thought of Dan there made him suddenly seem more adult and somewhat of a stranger. Somehow it added to his desolate feeling about the dog.

They broke camp at eleven after a long swim. "So long to Wilson Island!" Dan called out. Ahead lay a broad area of river broken by reeds and marsh. As they paddled along the northern shore they came in sight of the dam and the canal that would carry them into Glen Ross and lock number seven.

"Hi, there!" the lockmaster shouted. "I've been watching for you!"

"For us?" Dan called back. "Why?"

"Somebody was asking about you!"

Kip's heart leaped. The dog had been found! But the lockmaster's next words belied his hopes. "It was a family in a cruiser. Big forty-foot job with all the comforts of home."

"Dr. Morgan!" the boys sang out. "When did he come through?"

"Just yesterday. He's taking his time. The little girl's getting pretty tired of being cooped up on the boat so they stopped here for a while for her to run about. How long have you boys been on the go?"

"About a week," Kip said. And yet it seemed longer. Kip's Cove had been so far away and so much had happened since he had left it. It almost seemed like another person back there, a week ago, who had run up to the cedar grove to say a last good-bye to his dog.

"The doctor and his wife said to say hello to you and wish you good luck," the lockmaster told them. "He says to watch out for him next year around here."

"I'd like to think we could," Kip said. But next year was a long way off and Dan would be another year older then, and in high school. You didn't have much to do with kids in grade eight when you started to high school, Kip knew that.

"Let's eat here, Champ," Dan said. "We can sit up on the wall."

"Okay with me," Kip said.

They shared their lunch with the lockmaster. "This suits me," he said. "The wife and kids have gone to Frankford for the week-end, so I'm getting my own for a couple of days."

"Have one of our bananas for dessert," Dan offered. "You won't have much time for dishing up your own with Sunday traffic coming through here."

From the lock it was less than a mile to the point where the river took a sharp turn to the south, passing a gay group of tourist cabins. As three islands came into view, Dan said, "We should be coming on Rawdon Creek any minute now. You still want to go?"

"Sure I do!" Kip said. The thought of Edna and Stirling

was uppermost in his mind and he had almost forgotten about the dog. But only for a time. "The creek goes off on our port, doesn't it?"

"That's it. By the look of the map it's a fairly large creek, too. It shouldn't be hard to spot."

They came upon its mouth in another few minutes, and paddled in. From the beginning they found it tortuous in its course. They went slowly, uncertain as to what they might meet around the next bend.

"Jeepers!" Dan said. "This is like finding your way out of one of those mazes." They came at that moment into an area of thick sedge. "It looks like we've had it, Champ," he added. "I don't think we can go on."

"But there must be some way," Kip said.

"If we could find a parking place for the canoe," Dan said, "we could hoof it up to Stirling. It can't be that far."

"Let's do that," Kip agreed. "I'll bet I could walk for miles!"

"Wait a minute," Dan said. "Look over there. There's a little stream runs off the creek. I can see a barn beside it over the hill. Let's try there."

The smaller stream was deep enough for their canoe only for a few yards. As it came in sight of the barn its depth petered out to a mere few inches. Some black and white cattle were standing in it, placidly drinking.

The boys beached the canoe on the pebbles and walked up the slope towards the barn. Then they saw the old man watching them from under a heavily laden apple tree. "Hello," he said, "are you looking for somebody?"

"We'd like a place to leave the canoe," Dan said, "while we hike up the creek to Stirling."

"Stirling?" The old man looked surprised. "You know somebody there?"

"We know somebody that came from there," Kip said. "Edna Manser."

"Manser. Manser." The old man rubbed his wrinkled chin.

"I remember them. I went to school with her father. Frank Manser. Big fellow. Fair hair. No use your looking up the Mansers now. They sold up a few years back and left the place."

"Oh, we're just going for fun," Dan said. "How far do we have to travel?"

"Oh, quite a few miles up the creek," the old man replied. "My name's MacIntyre. Andrew MacIntyre. Been farming here for fifty years." He eyed the canoe. "You can leave your boat in the barn if you want to. It'll come to no harm there."

"Thanks a lot," Dan said.

The old man left at the sound of a church bell over the hill, and the boys turned to the canoe. "What do we need to take with us?" Kip asked, when they had it safely in the barn.

"It's warm enough," Dan said. "Let's make it a ground sheet and one blanket."

Kip looked surprised. "Are we going to stay the night?"

"If it's quite a few miles up the creek and after two now, we certainly won't be back before night," Dan reminded him. "If the house is still deserted the way Edna said it always used to be, maybe we can bunk in there."

Kip felt the funny prickly feeling down his back. Dan said there were no such things as ghosts but just the same, there had been the talk of the voice in the night calling the Indian name. And the house had been standing for years and years. There might be something to the tale after all. "I'll go where you go," he said at last, "wherever we set up for the night." And silently he wondered where that promise would take him when the night had come.

17. Edna's Ghost at Last

The path beside the creek was laced with brambles and wild berry bushes and the going was often painfully slow. In the late afternoon they stopped to paddle in the cold creek water. They even waded up to their knees in a wide pond where a young farm boy was fishing. "We should have brought our bathing trunks," Kip said. "What I couldn't do with a swim right about now!"

Dan looked around them at the water. It glistened in the afternoon sun among the folds of small hills. "This would be a super place to skate in winter," he said. "You could have a real wing-ding playing hockey here."

"That's for me," Kip said. The thought made him feel cool for a brief moment. "Who's your favourite team?"

"I don't think you can beat the Canadiens," Dan said. "I root for them a lot."

Kip smacked the water and a shower descended on Dan. "Traitor!" he laughed. "I'm a Maple Leaf fan and I'll bet they win the Stanley Cup this year!"

"Do you play hockey at home?" Dan asked.

Kip remembered the new house in the new neighbourhood. It seemed miles and weeks away. "I used to when we lived in the city," he said. "We played all winter on the school rink. Maybe I will when I get to know the kids around the new place." Then he remembered all the fun he had planned to have with Scout in the ravine behind the house and the empty feeling came back again.

"Sure," Dan said. "Let's get going now or we'll never make it in time for supper."

They trudged up a hill beside a snake fence on to the main street of Stirling at half-past five. They went down the steep hill towards the business section, and Kip smiled, remembering Edna hurtling down on her toboggan. As they passed the stores, he could see the mill pond below, overhung with gnarled willows.

"What are you limping for?" Dan asked.

"My feet are sore," Kip said. "I think I have blisters on both heels."

"I saw a drug store on the way down the hill," Dan remarked. "Let's go and get some band-aids."

But the door of the store was locked and the green shade drawn to the bottom. A woman called to them from a nearby garden. "It's closed on Sunday. The only place you'll find open is the restaurant."

"Thanks!" Dan sang out. "Say, Champ, that restaurant sounds like a good idea. I'm starved."

The waitress in the restaurant was a pretty girl about seventeen. She eyed them with curiosity as she brought their orders.

"Excuse me," Dan said, "but we're looking for an old place around here. People named White used to live there a long time ago. Do you know where it is?"

The girl gazed at them, obviously puzzled. "Yes, I do," she said. "It's on the way home over on the second line. You go up this street to the first one on your right. Turn right there and keep on walking. It's about a mile out." She smiled quickly, a charming, unaffected smile. "I'd be glad to show you the way if you like. I'll only be here another hour."

"Oh, we'll be all right," Kip broke in hastily. He did not want a girl showing them around. "Thanks all the same."

The boys found the band-aids at the counter and went down to a park bench to put them on. "It's all just the same as Edna's stories," Kip said. "It's just as if I'd been here before."

"I hope you'll know the old house when we get to it then," Dan grinned. "I'm counting on a floor to lie on for the night."

Kip knew it at once as the roof top came into view in the dusk. The road dipped here into a glade of huge elms. The house was set well back from the road and surrounded by a hedge run wild. Everything about the place mirrored age and neglect. The paint, grayed with weather, was peeling off four graceful wooden pillars before the arched front door. The broken green shutters on both windows were hanging loosely from their bolts. Even the stones in the walls had begun to crumble.

"There's a little cottage across the road," Kip said. "Do you think anybody lives there?"

"I don't think so," Dan said. "There are no curtains at the windows, and there are almost as many weeds in that garden as there are here." He pushed at the white gate rusted shut and overgrown with hedge. "Let's try to get this open and go round to the back. Perhaps we can find the window Edna went in. Remember?"

Kip saw it all at once: Edna shinnying down the drain pipe in the dead of night with her two brothers, the arrival at the wild garden of the old stone house here before him, Edna clambering over a window-sill to find the dark musty room clean-swept and tidy. And then the little bell ringing.

"Well, are you coming?" Dan was half-way round the house.

"Sure, I'll be there." The thorns of rose bushes run wild tore at his clothes as he went. The air was scented even now